"These new stories of William M[...] greatness invisibly. Like their pe[...] Tolstoy, Chekhov, Porter, and Welty, they slowly lure the reader into ironclad but transparent rooms. And soon we're held in the arms of a huge, benign host who wills us only an elegant pleasure, a deepened vision of our lost past, and a comprehending mercy now, in the smaller world of our diminished present."
—Reynolds Price

"Observant, witty, gracefully written . . . has that rare ability to take you by surprise. You read along, enjoying this visit to a small town in the early 1900's, and all of a sudden you stumble on something beautiful, or profoundly wise, or terribly sad."
—Josephine Humphreys,
The New York Times Book Review

WILLIAM MAXWELL has published six novels, two collections of short stories, an autobiographical memoir, and a book for children. For forty years he was a fiction editor at *The New Yorker*. From 1969 to 1972 he was president of the National Institute for Arts and Letters. He has received the Brandeis Creative Arts Award Medal and, for his novel *So Long, See You Tomorrow*, the American Book Award and the Howells Medal of the American Academy of Arts and Letters. He and his wife live in New York City.

ALSO BY WILLIAM MAXWELL

BILLIE DYER
AND OTHER STORIES

BY

WILLIAM MAXWELL

A PLUME BOOK

PLUME
Published by the Penguin Group
Penguin Books USA Inc., 375 Hudson Street,
New York, New York 10014, U.S.A.
Penguin Books Ltd, 27 Wrights Lane,
London W8 5TZ, England
Penguin Books Australia Ltd, Ringwood,
Victoria, Australia
Penguin Books Canada Ltd, 10 Alcorn Avenue,
Toronto, Ontario, Canada M4V 3B2
Penguin Books (N.Z.) Ltd, 182–190 Wairau Road,
Auckland 10, New Zealand

Penguin Books Ltd, Registered Offices:
Harmondsworth, Middlesex, England

Published by Plume, an imprint of New American Library,
a division of Penguin Books USA Inc.
This is a reprint of a hardcover edition published by Alfred A. Knopf, Inc.

First Plume Printing, February, 1993
10 9 8 7 6 5 4 3 2 1

"Billie Dyer," "Love," "The Man in the Moon," "My Father's Friends," "The Front and the
Back Parts of the House," and "The Holy Terror" were originally published in *The New
Yorker;* "With Reference to an Incident at a Bridge" was originally published in a volume
of writing honoring Eudora Welty and edited by Stuart Wright.

Ⓟ REGISTERED TRADEMARK—MARCA REGISTRADA

LIBRARY OF CONGRESS CATALOGING-IN-PUBLICATION DATA
Maxwell, William, 1908-
    Billie Dyer and other stories / by William Maxwell.
        p.   cm.
    Contents: Billie Dyer — Love — The man in the moon —With
reference to an incident at a bridge — My father's friends — The
front and the back parts of the house — The holy terror.
    ISBN 0-452-26950-4
    I. Title.   II. Series
[PS3525.A9464B55   1993]
813'.54—dc20
                                                    92-29110
                                                       CIP

Printed in the United States of America

CONTENTS

BILLIE DYER
AND OTHER STORIES

BILLIE DYER

If you were to draw a diagonal line down the state of Illinois from Chicago to St. Louis, the halfway point would be somewhere in Logan County. The county seat is Lincoln, which prides itself on being the only place named for the Great Emancipator before he became President. Until the elm blight reduced it in a few months to nakedness, it was a pretty late-Victorian and turn-of-the-century town of twelve thousand inhabitants. It had coal mines but no factories of any size. "Downtown" was, and still is, the courthouse square and stores that after a block or two in every direction give way to grass and houses. Which in turn give way to dark-green or yellowing fields that stretch all the way to the edge of the sky.

When Illinois was admitted into the Union there was not a single white man living within the confines of what is now the county line. That flat farmland was prairie grass, the hunting ground of the Kickapoo Indians. By 1833, under coercion, the chiefs of all the Illinois Indians had signed treaties ceding their territories to the United States. The treaties stipulated that they were to move their people west of the Mississippi River. In my childhood—that is to say, shortly before the First World War—arrowheads were turned up occasionally during spring plowing.

The town of Lincoln was laid out in 1853, and for more than a decade only white people lived there. The first Negroes were brought from the South by soldiers returning from the Civil War. They were carried into town rolled in a blanket so they would not be seen. They stayed indoors during the daytime and waited until dark for a breath of fresh air.

Muddy water doesn't always clear overnight. In the running conversation that went on above my head, from time to time a voice no longer identifiable would say, "So long as they know their place." A colored man who tried to attend the service at one of the Protestant churches was politely turned away at the door.

The men cleaned out stables and chicken houses, kept furnaces going in the wintertime, mowed lawns and raked leaves and did odd jobs. The women took in washing or cooked for some white family and now and then carried home a bundle of clothes that had become shabby from wear or that the children of the family had outgrown. I have been told by someone of the older generation that on summer evenings they would sit on their porches and sing, and that the white people would drive their carriages down the street where these houses were in order to hear them.

I am aware that "blacks" is now the acceptable form, but when I was a little boy the polite form was "colored people"; it was how they spoke of themselves. In speaking of things that happened long ago, to be insensitive to the language of the period is to be, in effect, an unreliable witness.

In 1953, Lincoln celebrated the hundredth anniversary of its founding with a pageant and a parade that outdid all other parades within living memory. The *Evening Courier* brought out a special edition largely devoted to old photographs and sketches of local figures, past and present, and the recollections of elderly people. A committee came up with a list of the ten most distinguished men that the town had produced. One was a Negro, William Holmes Dyer. He was then sixty-seven years old and living in Kansas City, and the head surgeon for all the Negro employees of the Santa Fe line. He was invited to attend the celebration, and did. There was a grand historical pageant with a cast of four hundred, and the Ten Most Distinguished Men figured in it. Nine of them were stand-ins with false chin whiskers, stovepipe hats, frock coats, and trousers that fastened under the instep. Dr. Dyer stood among them dressed in a dark-blue business suit, and four nights running accepted the honor that was due him.

Two years later, he was invited back again for a banquet of the Lincoln College Alumni Association, where he was given a citation for outstanding accomplishment in the field of medicine. While he was in town he called on the president of the college, who was a childhood friend of mine. "What did you talk about?" I asked, many years later, regretting the fact that so far as I knew I had never laid eyes on William Dyer. My friend couldn't remember. It was too long ago. "What was he like?" I persisted, and my friend, thinking carefully, said, "Except for the color of his skin he could have been your uncle. Or mine."

I have been looking at an old photograph of six boys playing soldier. They are somewhere between ten and twelve years old. There are trees behind them and grass; it is somebody's back yard. Judging by their clothes (high-buttoned double-breasted jackets, trousers cut off at the knee, long black stockings, high button shoes), the photograph was taken around 1900. One soldier has little flowers in his buttonhole. He and four of the others are standing at attention with their swords resting on their right shoulders. They can't have been real swords, but neither are they made of wood. The sixth soldier is partly turned but still facing the camera. As soon as the bulb is pressed he will lead the attack on Missionary Ridge. I assume they are soldiers in the Union Army, but who knows? Boys have a romantic love of lost causes. They must have had to stand unblinking for several minutes while the photographer busied himself under his black cloth. One of them, though I do not know which one, is Hugh Davis, whose mother was my Grandmother Blinn's sister. And one is Billie Dyer. His paternal grandmother was the child of a Cherokee Indian and a white woman who came from North Carolina in the covered-wagon days.

Billie Dyer's grandfather, Aaron Dyer, was born a slave in Richmond, Virginia, and given his freedom when he turned twenty-one. He made his way north to Springfield, Illinois, because it was a station of the Underground Railroad. It is thirty miles to the southwest of Lincoln, and the state capital. In Springfield, the feeling against slavery was strong; a runaway slave would be hidden sometimes for weeks until the owner who had traced him that far gave up and went home. Then Aaron Dyer would hitch up the horse and wagon he had been provided with, and at night the fugitive, covered with gunnysacks or an old horse blanket, would be driven along some winding wagon trail that led through the prairie. Clop, clop, clopty clop. Past farm buildings that were all dark and ominous. Fording shallow streams and crossing bridges with loose wooden floorboards that rumbled. Arousing the comment of owls. Sometimes Aaron Dyer sang softly to himself. Uppermost in his mind, who can doubt, was the thought of a hand pulling back those gunnysacks to see what was under them.

As for the fugitive concealed under the gunnysacks in the back of Aaron Dyer's wagon, whose heart beat wildly at the sound of a dog barking half a mile away, what he (or she) was escaping from couldn't have been better conveyed than in these complacent paragraphs from the Vicksburg, Mississippi, *Sun* of May 21, 1856:

> Any person, by visiting the slave depot on Mulberry Street, in this city, can get a sight of some of the latest importations of Congo negroes.
>
> We visited them yesterday and were surprised to see them looking so well, and possessing such intelligent countenances. They were very much like the common plantation negro—the only difference observable being the hair not kinking after the manner of the Southern darkey, while their feet, comparatively speaking, being very small, having a higher instep, and well-shaped in every respect.
>
> Some of the younger of these negroes are very large of their age, and are destined to attain a large growth. They all will make first-rate field hands, being easily taught to perform any kind of manual service. Their docility is remarkable, and their aptitude in imitating the manners and customs of those among whom they are thrown, is equally so.

On Decoration Day I saw, marching at the head of the parade, two or three frail old men who had fought in the war that freed them.

Two families lived in our house before my father bought it, in the early nineteen-hundreds. It had been there long enough for shade trees to grow around and over it. The ceilings were high, after the fashion of late-Victorian houses, and the downstairs rooms could not be closed off. My father complained, with feeling, about the coal bill. Like all old houses, it gave off sounds. The stairs creaked when there was no one on them, the fireplace chimneys sighed when the wind was from the east, and the sound, coming through the living-room floor, of coal being shoveled meant that Alfred Dyer was minding the furnace. Sometimes I went into the pantry and opened the cellar door and listened. The cellar stairs had no railing and the half-light was filtered through cobwebs and asbestos-covered heating pipes, and I never went down there. Sitting in the window seat in the library I would look out and see Mr. Dyer coming up the driveway to the cellar door. If he saw me playing outside he would say "Evening," in a voice much lower than any white man's. His walk was slow, as if he were dragging an invisible heaviness after him. It did not occur to me that the heaviness was simply that he was old and tired. Or even that he might have other, more presentable clothes than the shapeless sweater and baggy trousers I saw him in. I was not much better informed about the grown people around me than a dog or a cat would have been. I know now that he was born in Springfield, and could remember soldiers tramping the streets there with orders to shoot anybody who appeared to rejoice in the assassination of Abraham Lincoln. I have been told that for many years he took care of my Grandfather Blinn's horses and drove the family carriage. The horses and carriage were sold when my Uncle Ted persuaded my grandfather to buy a motorcar, and Mr. Dyer went to work for the lumber company.

Whoever it was that tried to worship where he wasn't wanted, it was not Alfred Dyer. He was for decades the superintendent of the African Methodist Episcopal Sunday school and led the choir. He knew the Bible so well, his daughter said, that on hearing any scriptural quotation he could instantly tell where it came from. As he was shaking the grates and setting the damper of our furnace, it seems likely that the Three Holy Children, Shadrach, Meshach, and Abednego, were more present to the eye of his mind than the little boy listening at the head of the cellar stairs.

After our house there were two more, and then Ninth Street dipped downhill, and at the intersection with Elm Street the brick pavement ended and the neighborhood took on an altogether different character. The houses after the intersection were not shacks, but they were not a great deal more. Grass did not grow in their yards, only weeds. There was usually a certain amount of flotsam and jetsam, whatever somebody more well-to-do didn't want and had found a way to get rid of. The Dyers' house was just around the corner on Elm Street. It was shaped like a shoebox and covered with green roofing paper. Elm Street was the dividing line between the two worlds. On either side of this line there were families who had trouble making both ends meet, but those who lived below the intersection didn't bother to conceal it.

As I sorted out the conversation of the grown people in my effort to get a clearer idea of the way things were, I could not help picking up how they felt, along with how they said they felt. While they agreed it was quite remarkable that Alfred Dyer's son William had got through medical school, at the same time they appeared to feel that in becoming a doctor he had imitated the ways of white people, as darkies were inclined to do, and done something that was not really necessary or called for, since there were, after all, plenty of white doctors. Apart from the doctors, the only things I can think of that the white people of Lincoln were at that time willing to share with the colored people were the drinking water and the cemetery.

Billie Dyer's mother was born in Sedalia, Missouri, the legal property of the wife of a general in the Union Army. Her father and mother ran away and were caught and returned, and the general put her father on the block and he was sold to someone in the South and never heard of again. When her children asked what the place where she was born was like, she told them she couldn't remember. And that nobody could come and take her away because the slaves were freed, all of them, a long time ago, and there would never be slaves again.

For things that are not known—at least not anymore—and that there is now no way of finding out about, one has to fall back on imagination. This is not the same thing as the truth, but neither is it necessarily a falsehood. Why not begin with the white lady? When he took the clean washing in his express wagon and knocked on her back door, she called him by his brother's name. She couldn't tell them apart. He didn't let on he wasn't Clarence.

The smell of laundry soap was the smell of home. With steam on the inside of the windows you couldn't always see out.

It was raining hard when school let out. Some children had raincoats and rubbers they put on. He ran all the way home, to keep from getting wet. He threw open the front door and fought his way through drying laundry to get to the kitchen, where his mother was, and said, "Mama, I'm starving," and she gave him a piece of bread and butter to tide him over.

With his hands folded and resting on the edge of the kitchen table, he waited for his father to say, "O Lord, we thank Thee for this bountiful sustenance. . . ." Pork chops. Bacon and greens. Sausages. Fried cornmeal mush. In summer coleslaw, and sweet corn and beets from the garden.

Saturday night his mother took the washtub down from its nail in the kitchen and made him stand in it while she poured soapy water over his head and scrubbed his back and arms. When she said, "Now that's what I call one clean boy!" he stepped out of the tub, his eyes still shut tight, and she threw a towel around him, and then it was Clarence's turn to have the inside of his ears dug at with a washrag.

In Sunday school, making the announcements and leading the singing, his father seemed twice as big as he did at home. Preacher told them about the hand: "Think of it, brothers and sisters and all you children, a hand—just a hand all by itself, no arm—*writing on the wall!*" For Sunday dinner they had chicken and dumplings, and sometimes there were little round egg yolks in the gravy.

He said, "Mama, I don't feel good," and her hand flew to his forehead. Then she went and got the bottle of castor oil and a big spoon, and said, "Don't argue with me, just open your mouth." Lying in bed with a fever, he listened to the old mahogany wall clock. Tick . . . and then tock . . . and then tick . . . and then tock . . . If he told his mother a lie she looked into his eyes and knew. Nothing bad could happen to them, because his father wouldn't let it happen. But if any of them talked back to him he got a switch from outside and whupped them. It wasn't even safe to say "Do I have to?"

His sister Mary didn't want to go to school, because the teacher made fun of her and said mean things. The teacher didn't like colored children. "Why can't I stay here and help you with the washing and ironing?" Mary said, and his mother said, "You'll be bending over a washtub soon enough. Go to school and show that white woman you aren't the stupid person she takes you for." After he finished his homework he helped Mary with hers. It was hard to get her to stop thinking about the teacher and listen to what he was telling her. "Nine and seven is not eighteen," he said patiently.

He fell asleep to the sound of his father's voice in the next room reading from the Bible. The patchwork quilts were old and thin, and in the middle of the night, when the fire in the kitchen stove died down, it was very cold in the house. One night when he went to bed it was December 31, 1899, and when he woke up he was living in a new century.

When he brought his monthly report card home from school his mother went and got her glasses and held it out in front of her and said, "Is that the best you can do?" Then she put the report card where they could all see it and follow his example.

If my Great-Aunt Ev's name was mentioned, my mother or my Aunt Annette would usually tell, with an affectionate smile, how she cooked with a book in her hand. They didn't mean a cookbook, and the implication was that her cooking suffered from it. She had graduated from the Cincinnati Conservatory of Music, and spoke several languages—which people in the Middle West at that time did not commonly do. The question "What will people think?" hardly ever crossed her mind. I have been told that my grandmother was jealous of her sister because my grandfather found her conversation so interesting. When her son Hugh Davis brought Billie Dyer home to play and they sat with their heads over the checkerboard until it was dark outside, she set an extra place at the table and sent one of the other children to ask Billie Dyer's mother if it was all right for him to stay for supper. Before long he was just one more child underfoot.

When he was alone with Hugh he thought only about what they were making or doing, but he never became so accustomed to the others that he failed to be alert to what they said. The eternal outsider, he watched how they ate and imitated it, and was aware of their moods. He learned to eat oysters and kohlrabi.

The first time they played hearts he left the hand that was

dealt him face-down on the table. "Pick up your cards," Hugh said. "You're holding up the game." The cards remained on the table. Mr. Davis said, "When your father told you you must never play cards, this isn't the kind of card-playing he meant. He meant playing for money. Gambling." Hugh, looking over his shoulder, helped him to arrange them in the proper suits. The hand that held the cards was small and thin and bluish brown on the outer side, pink on the inner.

At home, at the supper table, he said, "At the Davises' they—" and his sister Sadie said, "You like it so much at them white folks' house, why don't you go and live with them?"

He and Hugh Davis were friends all through grade school and high school. On Saturdays they went fishing together, and when they were old enough to be allowed to handle a gun they went hunting. Rabbits, mostly.

With a dry throat and weak knees and a whole row of Davises looking up at him solemnly, Hugh embarked upon the opening paragraphs of the high-school commencement address: "The Negro is here through no fault of his own. He came to us unwilling and in chains. He remains through necessity. He inhabits our shores today a test of our moral civilization. . . ." This must have been in the spring of 1904. I imagine there was a certain amount of shifting of feet on the part of the audience.

On his way to school, Billie Dyer had to pass an old house on Eighth Street that I remember mostly because there was a huge bed of violets by the kitchen door. I was never inside it but Billie Dyer was, and in that house his fate was decided. The house belonged to a man named David H. Harts, who was of my grandfather's generation. He had fought in the Civil War on the Union side, and been mustered out of the Army with the rank of captain. Though he had no further military service, he was always spoken of as Captain Harts. He was a member of the local bar association but applied himself energetically to many other things besides the practice of law. He was elected to the State Assembly, served a term as mayor of Lincoln, and ran for governor on the Prohibition ticket. His investments in coal mines, real estate, proprietary medicine, and interurban railroads had made him a wealthy man, but he was not satisfied to go on accumulating money; he wanted the men who worked for him to prosper also. Because coal mining was a seasonal occupation, he started a brick factory, so that the miners would have work during the summer months.

Everybody knew that Billie Dyer got very good grades in school, and Captain Harts's son John, who was four years older, would sometimes stop him on his way home from school. After a visit to the icebox they would sit on the back steps or under the grape arbor or in his room and talk. At some point in his growing up, John Harts had eye trouble sufficiently serious that the family doctor suggested he stop studying for a while and lead a wholly outdoor life. For months he lived all alone in a cabin in the woods. Every three or four days his father would drive out there with provisions. Occasionally he stayed the night. John Harts tried not to count the days between his father's visits or to wonder what time it was. Denied books, his hearing became more acute. He recognized the *swoosh* that meant a squirrel had passed from one tree to another. He heard, or didn't hear, the insects' rising and falling lament. The birds soon stopped paying any attention to him. He made friends with a toad. As he and his father sat looking into the fire his father told one story after another about his boyhood on a farm in Pennsylvania; about the siege of Vicksburg; about how when they were floating past what looked like an uninhabited island in the Mississippi they were fired on by Confederate infantry; about how when they were defending a trestle bridge some fifteen miles south of Jackson, Tennessee, Henry Fox, a sergeant in Company H, ran across the bridge in full view of the enemy and brought relief at the end of the day; how when they were stationed between the White and Arkansas rivers, a large number died of the malaria from the cypress swamp; how he was captured and used the year he spent in a military prison to study mathematics and science. Even though John Harts had heard some of these stories before, he never tired of hearing them. Lying awake, listening to the sound of his father's breathing, he knew there was no one in the world he loved so much. Sometimes his father brought his older brother and came again early the next morning, so that his brother would be in time for school. One Saturday he brought Billie Dyer. With their trousers rolled above the knee, they cleaned out the spring together. When it got dark, John Harts saw that Billie Dyer wished he was home. He talked him out of his fear of the night noises by naming them. There was a thunderstorm toward morning, with huge flashes of lightning, so that for an instant, inside the cabin, they saw each other as in broad daylight.

There is no record of any of this. It is merely what I think happened. I cannot, in fact, imagine it not happening. At any rate, it is known that when John Harts went away to college he wrote to Billie Dyer every week—letters of advice and encouragement that had a lasting effect on his life. At twenty-one, John Harts went to work as an engineer for the Chicago & Alton Railroad, and while he was operating a handcar somewhere on the line an unscheduled fast train sent the handcar flying into the air. People surmised that he didn't hear or see the locomotive until it was suddenly upon him, but in any case the flower of that family was laid to rest in Section A, Block 4, Lot 7 of the Lincoln Cemetery.

From time to time after that, Billie Dyer would put on his best clothes and pay a call on Captain Harts and his wife. When he graduated from high school, Captain Harts said to him, "And what have you decided to do with your life?" At that time, in Lincoln, it was not a question often asked of a Negro. Billie Dyer said, "I would like to become a doctor. But of course it is impossible." Captain Harts spoke to my grandfather and to several other men in Lincoln. How much they contributed toward Billie Dyer's education I have no way of knowing, but it does not appear to have been enough to pay all his expenses. It was thirteen years from the time he finished high school until he completed his internship at the Kansas City General Hospital. This could mean, I think, that he had to drop out of school again and again to earn the money he needed to go on with his studies. On the other hand, given the period, is it wholly beyond the realm of possibility that he should have come up against instructors who felt they were serving the best interests of the medical profession when they gave him failing marks for work that was in fact satisfactory, and forced him to take courses over again? In July, 1917, he came home ready to begin the practice of medicine, but America had declared war on Germany, the country was flooded with recruiting posters ("Uncle Sam Wants YOU!"), and they got to him. He was the first Negro from Lincoln to be taken into the Army.

2

In 1975, a Dallas real-estate agent named Jim Wood, wandering through a flea market in Canton, Texas, bought an Army-issue shaving kit, a Bible, and a manuscript. He collected shaving memorabilia and they were a single lot. Nothing is more improbable or subject to chance than the fate of objects. On the flyleaf of the Bible was written, in an old-fashioned hand, "To Dr. William H. Dyer from his father and mother." The manuscript appeared to be a diary kept by Dr. Dyer during the First World War. Months passed before Wood bothered to look at it. When he did, he became so interested that he read it three times in one sitting. He was convinced that Dr. Dyer must have made a significant contribution to the community he lived in, wherever that might be, and to the medical profession. So, for several years, with no other information than the diary contained, he tried to find Dr. Dyer or his heirs. Finally it occurred to him to write to the Lincoln public library.

The diary is a lined eight-by-twelve-inch copybook with snapshots and portrait photographs and postcards pasted in wherever they were appropriate. That it escaped the bonfire is remarkable; that it fell into the hands of so conscientious a man is also to be wondered at.

What seems most likely is that Dr. Dyer's wife was ill and that someone not a member of the family broke up the household. But then how did the diary get to Texas from Kansas City? It is eerie, in any case, and as if Dr. Dyer had gone on talking after his death, but about a much earlier part of his life. When the odds are so against something happening, it is tempting to look around for a supernatural explanation, such as that William Dyer's spirit, dissatisfied with the life he had led (the unremitting hard work, the selfless dedication to the sick and to the betterment of his race), longed for a second chance. Or, if not that, then perhaps wished to have remembered the eight months he spent in a half-destroyed country, where the French girls walked arm in arm with the colored soldiers and ate out of their mess pans with them, and death was everywhere.

On the first page of the diary he wrote, "With thousands

of others I decided to offer my life upon our Nation's altar as a sacrifice that Democracy might reign and Autocracy be forever crushed." In 1917, the age of public eloquence was not quite over, and when people sat down on a momentous occasion and wrote something it tended to be a foot or two above the ground.

Three hundred friends and neighbors were at the railroad station to see him off, on a Sunday afternoon, and he was kept busy shaking hands with those who promised to re-member him in their prayers. Somebody took a snapshot of him standing beside his father and mother. Alfred Dyer's rolled-brim hat and three-piece suit do not look as if they had been bought for someone else to wear and handed on to him when they became shabby. He is a couple of inches taller than his son. Both are fine-looking men.

From the diary: "Mother and Father standing there with tears in their eyes . . . when I kissed them and bade them farewell. . . . My eyes too filled with tears, my throat be-came full, and for miles as the train sped on I was unable to speak or to fix my mind upon a single thought."

His orders were to proceed to Fort Des Moines, a beauti-ful old Army post, at that time partly used as a boot camp for medical officers. He was disappointed with his quarters (a cold room in a stable) and did not at first see the need for a medical officer to spend four hours a day on the drill field.

After two months he was moved to Camp Funston, in Kansas. It was the headquarters of the 92nd Division, which was made up exclusively of Negro troops—the Army was not integrated until thirty-one years later, by executive order of Harry Truman. The barracks at Camp Funston were still being constructed, and thousands of civilian workmen poured into the camp every day, along with the draftees arriving by train from Kansas, Missouri, Colorado, Arizona, and Texas. He was assigned to the infirmary of the 317th

Ammunition Train, and when he was not treating the sick he weeded out recruits who were physically unfit for military service. The year before, he had fallen in love with a young woman named Bessie Bradley, who was teaching in a night school. His free weekends were spent in Kansas City, courting her. In January and February, an epidemic of cerebrospinal meningitis swept through the camp and kept him on his feet night and day until it subsided. In March, he got a ten-day furlough and took Bessie Bradley to Illinois and they were married.

At Camp Funston a bulletin was read to all the soldiers of the 92nd Division: "The Division Commander has repeatedly urged that all colored members of his commands, and especially the officers and noncommissioned officers, should refrain from going where their presence will be resented. In spite of this injunction, one of the Sergeants of the Medical Department has recently . . . entered a theater, as he undoubtedly had a legal right to do, and precipitated trouble by making it possible to allege race discrimination in the seat he was given. . . . Don't go where your presence is not desired."

This bulletin so stuck in his craw that he managed to get his hands on a copy of it, and it is written out in his diary in full, against some ultimate day of judging.

Early in June, the order came for the division to proceed to Camp Upton for embarkment overseas. Lieutenant Dyer tried to call his wife, but the troops were denied access to telegraph and telephone lines. The next day, the trains began pulling out of the camp. When his section drew into the railway station in Kansas City, he saw that there was an immense crowd. Without any hope whatever that his wife would be among them or that he would find her if she were, he put his head out of the train window and heard her calling to him.

The division was hurried from Camp Upton to the embarkation port at Hoboken and onto a magnificent old steamship that until the war had been carrying passengers back and forth across the Atlantic for the Hamburg-American line. It put out to sea with five thousand men on board, and when Lieutenant Dyer went on deck the next morning he saw that they had joined a great convoy of nine transport ships, two battle cruisers, and half a dozen destroyers. His ship was under the command of a colonel of a unit of the National Guard.

From the diary: "From the very start there was that feeling of prejudice brought up between the white and colored officers, for among the first orders issued were those barring colored officers from the same toilets as the whites, also barring them from the barber shop and denying colored officers the use of the ship's gymnasium." The sea was calm. The enlisted men were continually on the lookout for periscopes but saw instead flying fishes and porpoises and a whale that spouted. Lieutenant Dyer was assigned the daily sanitary inspection of certain compartments in the fore part of the ship, and the physical examination of six hundred men. Twice a day he submitted written reports to the ship's surgeon. On June 21st, shots were fired from all the surrounding ships at what proved to be a floating beer keg. A convoy of British destroyers brought them safely into the harbor at Brest. At nine-fifteen in the evening, when the men of his unit began to go ashore, the sun was still above the horizon. He was struck by the fact that the houses were all of stone and closely jammed together and very old, and by the expression of sadness on the faces of the French people. The women young and old all were in black and seemed to be in the deepest mourning. Four little tykes standing by the roadside sang, "Hail, hail, the gang's all here! What the hell do we care now," in perfect English. His unit marched three miles through the gathering darkness to a barracks that had been a prison camp during the time of Napoleon ("a terrible and dirty old place"), and stayed there four days awaiting orders. Twice he got a pass into the city. The French people were friendly when he went into a shop or attempted to converse with them. He sat down on a park bench and children congregated around him. Soon they were sitting on his knees and, pointing, told him the French words for his eyes, nose, ears, and neat mustache.

After three days and nights on a train and a nine-mile hike, his unit ended up in a camp outside a village forty-eight kilometers southeast of Poitiers. It was a beautiful region, untouched by the war. The men pitched their shelter tents in a level field, the officers were billeted in nearby manor houses. They were the first American troops in this region, and the natives fell in love with them and came visiting every day. ("With them there was *No Color Line*.") On Bastille Day, before a great crowd, the troops gave a demonstration of American sports—footraces, three-legged races, boxing, wrestling, and baseball.

On July 22nd, Companies B and C, with Lieutenant Dyer as their medical officer, had orders to proceed to Marseilles, where they were to procure trucks for the 317th Ammunition Train and drive them to the front. The officers rode first class, the enlisted men were crowded in boxcars but happy to be making the trip. It was the height of summer, and everywhere women and old men and children were working in the fields. He saw ox teams but no horses. And no young men. Along the tracks, leaning on their pickaxes and shovels as they waited for the train to pass by, were hundreds of German soldiers with "PG" printed in large white letters on the backs of their green coats. In the railway station of every city they came to he saw trainload after trainload of French soldiers headed for the front, where the

last great German offensive was being beaten back in the
second Battle of the Marne. His own train went east,
through vineyards. At Montluçon there was a stopover of
several hours, and an elderly English professor showed Lieutenant Dyer and another officer about the city and then took
them to the home of an aristocratic French family to meet a
pupil of his, a young lady who was very anxious to hear the
English spoken by Americans. After Lyons they turned
south, following the Rhône Valley. Every time the train
emerged from a tunnel, the men in the boxcars cheered. On
the fourth day, after emerging from a tunnel three miles
long, he saw the blue water of the Mediterranean.

The population of Marseilles was so mixed that it seemed
as if God had transplanted here a sample of His people from
all the kingdoms of the earth. Most of the men were in
uniform of some sort. The Algerian soldiers (many of them
"black as tar") with their little red skullcaps and the Hindus
in their turbans and loose garments were the strangest. How
in such garments could they fight in the trenches? As the
men of his company walked through the streets, people ex-
claimed, "Ah, Americans!" They were welcome in the best
hotels, the best theaters, everywhere. But it was a wicked
city. Sitting at a table in a sidewalk café, he saw many beautiful women who were clearly prostitutes.

No ammunition trucks were available, and so they traveled back through the same picturesque scenery until grad-
ually it became less picturesque and the farms less well
tended. At Is-sur-Tille, where there was a huge American
advance-supply base, they spent the greater part of the day
on a siding. That night, no lights were allowed in the railroad cars, and from this they knew they were approaching
the front. The 92nd Division headquarters was now at Bour-
bonne-les-Bains, three hundred kilometers southeast of
Paris. As Lieutenant Dyer stepped down onto the station

platform, the first officers he saw were from his old Camp Funston unit. He reported to the division surgeon and was put on duty in a camp just outside the city.

During the week that his unit remained here, their lockers were taken from them, their equipment was reduced to fifty pounds, and they were issued pistols and ammunition. On the twelfth of August they left the camp in a long convoy of motortrucks, which traveled all afternoon and night and stopped the next morning in the pretty little village of Bruyères. Here they were quartered in an old barracks that turned out to be comfortable enough when put in sanitary condition. Bruyères was a railroad terminal where American and French divisions and supplies were unloaded for the front. Aside from some humiliating divisional orders, which the diary does not go into, his stay there was pleasant. In the evening he walked out on the hills beyond the town and watched the anti-aircraft guns firing at German bombers. The distant flashes of cannons were like sheet lightning on the horizon.

Toward the end of August, on a night of the full moon—though it was almost totally obscured by clouds—he sat in a crowded truck with a rifle between his knees and his eyes focused on the dim road ahead. The convoy drove without lights, and they kept passing Army vehicles that had broken down or had slid off the road into a ditch, and infantrymen who, because of fatigue and the weight of their packs, had fallen out of the line to rest. He gave up counting the houses with their roofs gone or that were completely destroyed. The whole countryside had a look of desolation. At three o'clock in the morning, the convoy arrived at a silent and largely destroyed town. The truck he was riding in drove up an alley and stopped. He and two other officers lay down in front of a building that appeared to be intact and, using the stone doorstep for a pillow, fell asleep from exhaustion. In the morning, the occupants of the building, leaving for work, stepped over them. He got up and asked where they were and was told that it was Raon-l'Étape, in the Vosges.

For two days the American troops bivouacked in a wood, with German planes lingering high in the air above them in spite of the anti-aircraft guns. Then they were moved back to the town, and that night an enemy bomber dropped four bombs on the place where they had camped, creating terrific explosions. He was billeted at the house of a Mme. Crouvé-sier, whose two sons were in a prison camp in Germany. Working chiefly at night, because the Germans had occupied this area for three weeks in 1914 and knew the roads perfectly, the 317th moved ammunition of all calibers from the woods where it was hidden to four regiments of American infantry and a French artillery unit that was operating with them. The town was full of graves—in back yards, in gardens, everywhere. While he stood looking at an enemy observation balloon it suddenly went up in a fiery cloud. A German plane was brought down at Raon-l'Étape and the dead aviators were given a military funeral, which he attended.

After nearly a month here, he again found himself in a convoy, which drove all day and at 11 p.m. stopped along the roadside for the night. The truck he was riding in was so crowded that he got out and slept on the ground, wrapped in his blankets, and was awakened two hours later by a downpour. He moved under the truck, but his blankets became so wet that he gave up and moved back into the truck, and with the rain trickling down the back of his neck finished out the night.

Two days later, they reached their destination—the Argonne Forest. There were no accommodations for them, not even water to drink or to cook with, and the mud everywhere was over their shoe tops. They pitched their tents under bushes and trees to keep from being observed by the enemy airplanes constantly flying over. The companies of the 317th were detailed to handle supplies at a nearby rail-head and deliver hundreds of horses to units at the front. ("While camped in this wet, filthy woods, many of our boys became ill from the dampness, cold, and exposure, thereby causing me much work and worry, caring for them.") Division headquarters issued a bulletin that Negro soldiers would be used to handle mustard-gas cases, because they were less susceptible than whites. ("Why is the Negro less susceptible to mustard gas than the whites? *No one can answer.*") On September 25th, a very heavy bombardment began, and it kept up for thirty-six hours without a stop. ("The old woods . . . trembled as if by earthquake, the flashes of the cannon lighted up the inside of our tents, and our ears were deafened.") Lieutenant Dyer went several times to the American evacuation hospital, a quarter of a mile away, and saw a continuous stream of ambulances bringing wounded soldiers to it from the front. The dead were also being brought back, on trucks, piled like cordwood and dripping blood.

They moved on, to Sainte-Menehould, forty-seven kilo-meters west of Verdun, and were billeted on the top floor of a French barracks. From their windows they could see the lines. The area was full of American soldiers plodding along under their heavy packs. Standing on the top of a hill, he could make out the Argonne Forest, with smoke hanging over it. Big guns were belching from all the surrounding hills. The 317th worked round the clock. With no tall trees and only one other building near it, the barracks made a fine target. ("All through the night the fighting kept up and though scared stiff and expecting to be blown to atoms at any moment I finally fell asleep.")

On the seventh of October, Companies B and C left

Sainte-Menehould. The trucks drove south and east all day, in a driving rain, with a cold wind. In many places the road was camouflaged with green burlap supported on wire fences sometimes fifteen feet high and thickly interwoven with bushes and small trees. They passed through towns where not one house was standing whole and there was no longer any civilian population. A ruin next to a graveyard meant that there had been a church on this spot. Even the grass was burned up. ("At 5 p.m. we reached the city of Commercy, where we had orders to spend the night. We were taken to a French barracks where there were fairly good quarters for officers and men. We had just gotten comfortably located in the building, quite glad to get out of the inclement weather, and were preparing to eat, when another order came for the ammunition train to move on. . . . The rain fell and the wind blew and I sat on an open truck helping the driver watch the road to prevent running over an embankment, which would probably have meant our death. . . . All night long we traveled on, wondering what our destination would be and why we should be ordered to move on such a night.") At four in the morning, the convoy stopped in the village of Belleville. Cold, wet, and hungry, he got down and stomped on the ground, hoping to generate a little body heat. At daybreak a feed cart came by and the driver pitched them a few steaks left over from the breakfast of a labor battalion.

Belleville was so protected by the surrounding hills that the shells from the enemy guns at Metz almost never reached it. Lieutenant Dyer and another lieutenant were billeted in the ancient, dilapidated house of an elderly French couple. The officers' second-floor room had one small window. On the walls and rafters were a few traces of whitewash. There was a fireplace and two immense wardrobes. Over their heads was a loft full of straw, in which rats, mice, and birds nested. Sometimes their frisking sent chaff down on the faces of the two men. The beds were good. Lying in his, Lieutenant Dyer listened to the sound of the German planes overhead and tried to gauge, by the whine of a falling shell, whether the explosion would be a safe distance away.

He set up his infirmary in a small electrical plant. Because of the constant cold and rainy weather, there was a great deal of sickness among the colored troops. (Not once does he speak of what in America was called "the Spanish flu," but it was that, undoubtedly, that the men in his company were coming down with.)

Companies A, D, E, F, and G and their artillery, in training in the South of France since July, arrived in Belleville. ("Major Howard, my commanding officer from whom I had been separated about four months, called to see me . . . and complimented me on my good work, saying he had seen the Division Surgeon and not one complaint was made against me. During the whole month of October we labored on, hearing much talk of peace and were very anxious for the final drive, which would end forever Autocracy and give Democracy the right to reign. On the morning of November 8th, however, while we were in the midst of our activities, a terrible thing occurred at Belleville. . . . A colored boy who had been convicted of rape in August was hanged or lynched in an open field not far from my infirmary. The execution was a military order, but so openly and poorly carried out that it was rightly termed a lynching.")

The next day, the drive against Metz began, and two days later, while tremendous barrages were being laid down by the artillery in support of the infantries' advances, the news reached them that Germany had signed an armistice. As everywhere else in the Western world, bells rang, whistles blew, people shouted for joy.

On December 6th, he and another officer climbed into a

truck and after a two-hour ride through no-man's-land arrived in Metz. He found it untouched by the fighting and
the most beautiful city he had seen in France. The buildings
were modern; the streets were wide and well paved and
lighted with gas or electricity; there were streetcars riding
up and down. But the people were cold and unfriendly to
them, and spoke German mostly, and it was clear from the
way a pack of children followed them in the street that they
had never seen a Negro before.

On the night of December 15th, he was awakened by the
orderly boy. In a heavy fog, a passenger train from Metz
had plowed into a troop train full of happy French soldiers
returning home from the front. It was a dreadful sight. The
cars were telescoped and splintered, and the bodies of the
dead and dying were pinned under the wreckage. The rest
of the night he dressed wounds and put splints on broken
arms and legs.

Three days later, the 317th began to leave Belleville. Now
on foot, now in trucks or trains, they moved westward toward their port of embarkation. Sometimes he slept on
straw, in dirty makeshift buildings that had been occupied
by other soldiers before them and were infested with lice.
For two days and nights he rode in a crowded railway coach
with the rain dripping down on him from a leak in the ceiling. On Christmas Eve, in the ancient village of Domfront,
in Normandy, the medical unit stood about in the rain and
snow until 3 a.m., waiting to be billeted by a captain who,
it turned out, had forgotten about them. Shivering in the
cold, he remembered the Biblical text: *Foxes have holes and the
fowls of the air have nests, but the Son of Man hath not where to
lay his head.*

The people of Domfront were extremely hospitable, and
the colored troops reciprocated by being on their best behavior. He was kept busy inspecting them daily for vermin and

acute infections, but he found time to visit the places of historical interest and had his picture taken at the foot of the castle wall. Then he himself came down with influenza and had to be looked after by the men of his medical corps.

Late in January, his unit was ordered to proceed to the delousing station at Le Mans. The weather was cold, and there was a light snow on the ground. They reached Le Mans at eleven o'clock at night, after a twelve-hour ride. When he climbed down out of the truck, he had difficulty walking. He took off his boots and discovered that his feet were frozen. ("For a week thereafter, my feet were so swollen and blistered that I was unable to wear a shoe or leave my quarters.") During the two weeks he spent at the delousing camp he ran into several boys from Springfield that he knew. They had seen hard service with the 8th Illinois Infantry and showed it.

The unit made its final train journey from Le Mans to Brest, where thousands of soldiers were now crowded into the area around the port. The barracks were long wooden shacks with a hall running through the middle and small rooms opening off it. The only heat came from two stoves, one at either end of the hall. ("The weather was extremely damp and chilly at Brest, the raw wind off the ocean penetrating to the marrow.") There was more sickness.

On the morning of February 22nd, the 317th marched to the port. They had been informed by a bulletin from headquarters that if there was any disorder in the ranks they would be sent back to camp and detained indefinitely. Their packs uniformly rolled, their guns and shoes polished, they moved in utter silence like a funeral procession. The *Aquitania* rode at anchor in the harbor, and they were loaded onto small barges and ferried out to it. Lieutenant Dyer's cabin had mahogany fittings and a private bathroom. There were taps for fresh water and salt water, and the soap did not smell of disinfectant. While he was in the tub soaking, the room began to rock, and he realized that they had put out to sea. There is more, but why not leave him there, as lighthearted as he was probably ever going to be.

3

Of Dr. Dyer's roughly forty years of medical practice in Kansas City there is no record that I know of. The pattern of his days must have been regular and consistent. I picture him with a stethoscope in the pocket of his white coat and a covey of internes crowding around him.

In 1946, Hugh Davis, who was then living in California and an architect, came with his wife to Lincoln for a family visit. While he was there, he got Dr. Dyer's address and wrote to him to say that they would be going through Kansas City with a stopover of several hours and would like to see him. The answer was an invitation to dinner. There had been no communication between them for a good many years. The walls of the Dyers' Kansas City apartment were covered with Bessie Dyer's paintings, which the Davises liked very much. She was self-taught, with the help of a book that she got from the public library. They all sat down to a full Thanksgiving dinner, though actually Thanksgiving was about ten days away. And the friendship simply picked up where it had left off.

Two years later, when the Dyers went out to California, they were entertained at Hugh and Esther Davis's house in Palo Alto, along with a medical acquaintance the Dyers were staying with. My younger brother was also invited. He had just come out of the Army after a tour of duty in Germany, and was enrolled in law school at Stanford. He remembers Dr. Dyer as soft-spoken and very friendly, if a trifle guarded. He seemed to want, and need, to talk about the situation of educated Negroes in America—how they are not always comfortable with members of their own race, with whom they often have little or nothing in common, and are not accepted by white people whose tastes and interests they share. He was neither accusing nor bitter about this, my brother said. My brother mentioned the fact that Dr. Dyer's mother had helped take care of him when he was a baby, and Dr. Dyer was pleased that my brother remembered her. Three or four times he interrupted the conversation to say "I never expected to sit down to dinner with a grandson of Judge Blinn."

Hugh Davis's widow let me see a few of Dr. Dyer's letters to him written between 1955 and 1957. They are about politics (he was an ardent Republican), the hydrogen bomb, various international crises, a projected high-school reunion that never took place, his wife's delicate health, and—as one would expect of any regular correspondence—the weather. They are signed "Your friend, Billie Dyer." In each letter there is some mention of his professional activity—never more than a sentence, as a rule; taken together they give a very good picture of a man working himself to death.

In January, 1956, at which time he was seventy years old, he wrote, "I suppose I should apologize for not having written you sooner but believe it or not, I am now working harder and with longer hours than ever before. Silly, you say, well I quite agree but the occasion is this. In the last four months I have been put on the staffs of three of the major hospitals in our city. I thought at first it was an honor but with the increase in activities which such appointments entail, my work has increased twofold. Since it is the first time that one of my race has had such appointments, I have been working diligently to make good, thereby keeping those doors open." He was still acting as a surgeon for the Santa Fe Railroad, and also for the Kansas City, Kansas, police department.

Three months later he wrote, "Since I have taken on new

hospital assignments I have been working much too hard. I was in Chicago this week three days attending the Convention of American Association of Railway Surgeons and derived great benefit from the lectures and demonstrations on recent advances in medicine and surgery."

In June he spent a couple of weeks in the wilds of Minnesota fishing and had a glorious time, though the fishing was poor. In August he wrote, "I am still working as hard as ever altho my physical resistance is not what it used to be & I find I must resort to more frequent short periods of rest."

The letter he wrote in November is largely about the suppression of the Hungarian uprising: "My heart goes out to those people. I was in France in the First World War & I saw refugees going down the roads with a little cart pulled by a donkey & all of their earthly possessions piled high on it. They had been driven from their homes by the advancing German Armies & it was a pitiful sight to behold." He also mentions the fact that the vision in his right eye is somewhat impaired because of a small cataract, and adds, "I am still working at a tremendous pace but realize that I must soon slow down."

In March of the following year he wrote, "I hardly have time to breathe. Indeed I know that at my age I should not be trying such a pace but having broken thru a barrier which was denied me so many years . . ."

In July he wrote, "I too am having my troubles with a nervous dermatitis which all of the skin specialists tell me is due to overwork. . . . I am planning on spending a couple of weeks on the lakes in northern Minnesota for I am very tired and need a rest."

And in August: "I will be 71 years old the 29th of this month and am in fairly good health for an old man of my years. I therefore thank the good Lord for His blessings. . . . I thought I would get out to California this summer but

I had to buy a new car, so will have to defer my visit another year. . . . I agree with you that Ike has been a little wishy washy since he has been in the White House. It seems that he speaks softly but does not carry the big stick like Teddy Roosevelt once did. Hugh I shall never forget the political rallies and torchlight processions they had in Lincoln when we were boys. We don't see anything like that any more, and when the circuses came to town with their big parades. How I pity the generations of kids today, who are denied such thrills. Remember the old swimming hole in Kickapoo Creek where we used to swim naked and have so much fun. Hugh those were the days."

In January there was a notice in the Lincoln *Evening Courier:* "Dr. William Dyer, a native of Lincoln, was found dead in his car after an automobile accident at Kansas City, Kan., Tuesday morning. He apparently suffered a heart attack while driving."

There have been at least three histories of Logan County. The first was published in 1878 by a firm that went through the state doing one county after another. It has portrait engravings and brief biographies of the leading citizens, for which they must have paid something. The style is a little like First and Second Chronicles: "Michael and Abram Mann, John Jessee and Thomas Sr., Lucas and Samuel Myers were from Ohio and are now in their graves." Many natural wonders that the early settlers remembered found their way into this book—prairie fires so numerous that at night they lighted up the whole circuit of the horizon. And mirages. Also extreme hardships—the ague, caused by hunting their horses in the wet grass, and a drop in the temperature so great and so sudden, on a rainy December afternoon in 1836, that men on horseback were frozen to the saddle. And primitive artifacts, such as a door with wooden hinges, a wooden lock, and a buckskin drawstring.

Another history, published in 1911, was the work of a local man and is overburdened with statistics. The most recent is a large book—nine by twelve—heavy to hold in the hand and bound in red Leatherette. The likeness of Abraham Lincoln is on the cover, embossed in gold, as if somewhere in the Afterlife his tall shade had encountered King Midas. There are hundreds of photographs of people I don't know and never heard of, which is not to be wondered at since we moved away from Lincoln in 1923, when I was fourteen years old.

Someone who had never lived there might conclude from this book that the town had no Negroes now or ever. Except for the group pictures of the Lincoln College athletic teams, in which here and there a dark face appears among the lighter ones, there are no photographs of black men and women. And though there are many pictures of white churches of one denomination or another, there is no picture of the African Methodist Episcopal Church—only a column of text, in which the buildings it occupied and the ministers who served it are listed. And these sentences: "Mr. Arian [surely Aaron misremembered?] Dyer and wife Harriet moved here from Springfield, Illinois, in 1874. . . . The sinners in Lincoln found the hope in Christ and joined the church. Among them were Alfred Dyer and wife Laura. . . ."

I go through the book looking for the names that figured so prominently in the conversation of my elders and find almost none. And realize that the place to look for them is the cemetery. The past is always being plowed under. There is a page of pictures of the centennial parade, but nowhere are the names of the Ten Most Distinguished Men called to mind. What is one to think if not that the town, after cele-

brating its hundredth birthday, was done with history and
its past, and ready to live, like the rest of America, in a
perpetual present?

In the index I found "Dyer, William, 90, 202." Both ref-
erences turned out to be concerned with a white man of that
name.

LOVE

Miss Vera Brown, she wrote on the blackboard, letter by letter in flawlessly oval Palmer method. Our teacher for the fifth grade. The name might as well have been graven in stone.

As she called the roll, her voice was as gentle as the expression in her beautiful dark brown eyes. She reminded me of pansies. When she called on Alvin Ahrens to recite and he said, "I know but I can't say," the class snickered but she said, "Try," encouragingly, and waited, to be sure that he didn't know the answer, and then said, to one of the hands waving in the air, "Tell Alvin what one-fifth of three-eighths is." If we arrived late to school, red-faced and out of breath and bursting with the excuse we had thought up on the way, before we could speak she said, "I'm sure you couldn't help it. Close the door, please, and take your seat." If she kept us after school it was not to scold us but to help us past the hard part.

Somebody left a big red apple on her desk for her to find when she came into the classroom, and she smiled and put it in her desk, out of sight. Somebody else left some purple asters, which she put in her drinking glass. After that the presents kept coming. She was the only pretty teacher in the school. She never had to ask us to be quiet or to stop throwing erasers. We would not have dreamed of doing anything that would displease her.

Somebody wormed it out of her when her birthday was. While she was out of the room the class voted to present her with flowers from the greenhouse. Then they took another vote and sweet peas won. When she saw the florist's box waiting on her desk, she said, "Oh?"

"Look inside," we all said.

Her delicate fingers seemed to take forever to remove the ribbon. In the end, she raised the lid of the box and ex- claimed.

"Read the card!" we shouted.

Many Happy Returns to Miss Vera Brown, from the Fifth Grade, it said.

She put her nose in the flowers and said, "Thank you all very, very much," and then turned our minds to the spelling lesson for the day.

After school we escorted her downtown in a body to a special matinée of D. W. Griffith's *Hearts of the World*. She was not allowed to buy her ticket. We paid for everything.

We meant to have her for our teacher forever. We in- tended to pass right up through the sixth, seventh, and eighth grades and on into high school taking her with us. But that isn't what happened. One day there was a substi- tute teacher. We expected our real teacher to be back the next day but she wasn't. Week after week passed, and the substitute continued to sit at Miss Brown's desk, calling on us to recite and giving out tests and handing them back with grades on them, and we went on acting the way we had when Miss Brown was there because we didn't want her to come back and find we hadn't been nice to the substitute. One Monday morning she cleared her throat and said that Miss Brown was sick and not coming back for the rest of the term.

In the fall we had passed on into the sixth grade and she

was still not back. Benny Irish's mother found out that she was living with an aunt and uncle on a farm a mile or so beyond the edge of town, and told my mother, who told somebody in my hearing. One afternoon after school Benny and I got on our bikes and rode out to see her. At the place where the road turned off to go to the cemetery and the Chautauqua grounds, there was a red barn with a huge circus poster on it, showing the entire inside of the Sells-Floto Circus tent and everything that was going on in all three rings. In the summertime, riding in the back seat of my father's open Chalmers, I used to crane my neck as we passed that turn, hoping to see every last tiger and flying-trapeze artist, but it was never possible. The poster was weather-beaten now, with loose strips of paper hanging down.

It was getting dark when we wheeled our bikes up the lane of the farmhouse where Miss Brown lived.

"You knock," Benny said as we started up on the porch.

"No, you do it," I said.

We hadn't thought ahead to what it would be like to see her. We wouldn't have been surprised if she had come to the door herself and thrown up her hands in astonishment when she saw who it was, but instead a much older woman opened the door and said, "What do you want?"

"We came to see Miss Brown," I said.

"We're in her class at school," Benny explained.

I could see that the woman was trying to decide whether she should tell us to go away, but she said, "I'll find out if she wants to see you," and left us standing on the porch for what seemed like a long time. Then she appeared again and said, "You can come in now."

As we followed her through the front parlor I could make out in the dim light that there was an old-fashioned organ like the kind you used to see in country churches, and linoleum on the floor, and stiff uncomfortable chairs, and family portraits behind curved glass in big oval frames.

The room beyond it was lighted by a coal-oil lamp but seemed ever so much darker than the unlighted room we had just passed through. Propped up on pillows in a big double bed was our teacher, but so changed. Her arms were like sticks, and all the life in her seemed concentrated in her eyes, which had dark circles around them and were enormous. She managed a flicker of recognition but I was struck dumb by the fact that she didn't seem glad to see us. She didn't belong to us anymore. She belonged to her illness.

Benny said, "I hope you get well soon."

The angel who watches over little boys who know but they can't say it saw to it that we didn't touch anything. And in a minute we were outside, on our bicycles, riding through the dusk toward the turn in the road and town.

A few weeks later I read in the Lincoln *Evening Courier* that Miss Vera Brown, who taught the fifth grade in Central School, had died of tuberculosis, aged twenty-three years and seven months.

Sometimes I went with my mother when she put flowers on the graves of my grandparents. The cinder roads wound through the cemetery in ways she understood and I didn't, and I would read the names on the monuments: Brower, Cadwallader, Andrews, Bates, Mitchell. In loving memory of. Infant daughter of. Beloved wife of. The cemetery was so large and so many people were buried there, it would have taken a long time to locate a particular grave if you didn't know where it was already. But I know, the way I sometimes know what is in wrapped packages, that the elderly woman who let us in and who took care of Miss Brown during her last illness went to the cemetery regularly and poured the rancid water out of the tin receptacle that was sunk below the level of the grass at the foot of her grave, and filled it with fresh water from a nearby faucet and arranged the flowers she had brought in such a way as to please the eye of the living and the closed eyes of the dead.

THE MAN
IN THE MOON

In the library of the house I grew up in there was a box of photographs that I used to look through when other forms of entertainment failed me. In this jumble there was a postcard of my mother's brother, my Uncle Ted, and a young woman cozying up together in the curve of a crescent moon. I would have liked to believe that it was the real moon they were sitting in, but you could see that the picture was taken in a photographer's studio. Who she was it never occurred to me to ask. Thirty or forty years later, if his name came up in conversation, women who were young at the same time he was would remark how attractive he was. He was thin-faced and slender, and carried himself well, and he had inherited the soft brown eyes of the Kentucky side of the family.

In the small towns of the Middle West at that time—I am speaking of, roughly, the year 1900—it was unusual for boys to be sent away to school. My uncle was enrolled in a military academy in Gambier, Ohio, and flunked out. How much education he had of a kind that would prepare him for doing well in one occupation or another I have no idea. I would think not much. Like many young men born into a family in comfortable circumstances, he felt that the advantages he enjoyed were part of the natural order of things. What the older generation admired and aspired to was dignity, resting on a firm basis of accomplishment. I think what my uncle had in mind for himself was the life of a classy gent, a spender—someone who knows, from experience, which pleasures to seek out and which to avoid as not worth the bother, and who gives off the glitter of privilege. And he behaved as if this kind of life was within his reach. Which it wasn't. There was a period—I don't know how long it was, perhaps a few months, perhaps a year or so—when if he was strapped and couldn't think of anybody to put the bite on, he would write out a check to himself and sign it with the name of one of his sisters or of a friend.

I don't think anything on earth would have induced my father to pass a bad check, but then his family was poor when he was a child, and lived on the street directly behind the jail. Under everything he did, and his opinions about human behavior, was the pride of the self-made man. He blamed my uncle's shameless dodges on his upbringing. When my Grandfather Blinn would try to be strict with his son, my father said, my grandmother would go behind his back and give Teddy the money. My grandmother's indulgence, though it may have contributed to my uncle's lapses from financial probity, surely wasn't the only cause of them. In any case, the check forging didn't begin until both my grandparents were dead.

My grandfather was brought up on a cattle farm in Vermont not far from the Canadian border. He left home at sixteen to work as a bookkeeper in a pump factory in Cincinnati. Then he began to read law in a law office there. More often than not, he read on an empty stomach, but he mastered Blackstone's *Commentaries* and Chitty's *Pleadings*, and shortly before his twenty-first birthday (nobody thinking to inquire into his age, which would have prevented it) he was admitted to the bar. What made him decide to move farther west to Illinois I don't know. Probably there were already too many lawyers in Ohio. When he was still in his early thirties he tried to run for Congress on the Republican ticket and was nosed out by another candidate. Some years later the nomination was offered to my grandfather at a moment when there was no serious Democratic opposition, and he chose not to run because it would have taken him away from the practice of law. By the time he was forty he had a considerable reputation as a trial lawyer, and eventually he argued cases before the Supreme Court. Lawyers admired him for his ability in the courtroom, and for his powers of close reasoning. People in general saw in him a certain largeness of mind that other men didn't have. From the way my mother spoke of him, it was clear that—to her—there never had been and never could be again a man quite so worthy of veneration. My uncle must often have felt that there was no way for him to stand clear of his father's shadow.

Because my grandfather had served a term on the bench of the Court of Claims, he was mostly spoken of as Judge Blinn. His fees were large but he was not interested in accumulating money and did not own any land except the lot his house stood on. He was not at all pompous, but when he left his office and came home to his family he did not entirely divest himself of the majesty of the law, about which he felt so deeply. From a large tinted photograph that used to hang over the mantelpiece in my Aunt Annette's living room, I know that he had a fine forehead, calm gray eyes, and a drooping mustache that partly concealed the shape of his mouth.

There were half a dozen imposing houses in Lincoln but my grandfather's house wasn't one of them. It stood on a quiet elm-shaded street, and was a two-story flat-roofed house with a wide porch extending all across the front and around the sides. It was built in the eighteen-seventies and is still there, if I were to drive down Ninth Street. It is well over a hundred years old—what passes for an old house in the Middle West. My father worked for a fire-insurance company and was gone three days out of the middle of the week, drumming up business in small-town agencies all over the state. We lived across the street from my grandfather's house. Though I haven't been in it for sixty years, I can still move around in it in my mind. Sliding doors—which I liked to ease in and out of their recesses—separated the back parlor, where the family tended to congregate around my grandmother's chair, from the front parlor, where nobody ever sat. There it was always twilight because the velvet curtains shut out the sun. If I stood looking into the pier glass between the two front windows I saw the same heavy walnut and mahogany furniture in an even dimmer light. Whether this is an actual memory or an attempt on the part of my mind to adjust the past to my feelings about it I am not altogether sure. The very words "the past" suggest lowered window shades and a withdrawal from brightness of any kind. Orpheus in the Underworld. The end of my grandfather's life—he died horribly, of blood poisoning, from a ferret bite—cast a shadow backward over what had gone before, but in point of fact it was not a gloomy house, and the life that went on in it was not withdrawn or melancholy.

My Aunt Edith was the oldest. Then came my mother. Then Annette. Between Annette and my uncle there was another child, who didn't live very long. My grandmother was morbidly concerned for my uncle's safety when he was little, and Annette was told that she must never let him out of her sight when they were playing together. She was not much older than he was, and used to have nightmares in which something happened to him. They remained more or less in this relationship to each other during the whole of their lives.

My mother and her sisters had a certain pride of family, but it had nothing to do with a feeling of social superiority, and was, actually, so unexamined and metaphysical that I never understood the grounds for it. It may have been something my grandmother brought with her from Kentucky and passed on to her children. That branch of the family didn't go in for genealogy, and the stories that have come down are vague and improbable.

When I try the name Youtsey on a Southerner, all the response I ever get is a blank look. There appear to have been no statesmen in my grandmother's family, no colonial governors, no men or women of even modest distinction. That leaves money and property. My grandmother's father, John Youtsey, owned a hundred acres of land on the Licking River, where he raised strawberries for the markets of Cincinnati. He was also a United States marshal—that is to say, he had been appointed to carry out the wishes of the judicial district in which he lived, and had duties similar to those of a sheriff. Three of his sons fought in the Civil War, on the side of the North. Shortly before the war broke out, he began to build a new house with bricks fired on the place. I saw it once. I was taken there by one of my mother's cousins. The farm had passed out of the family and was now owned by a German couple. My grandmother used to take her children to Kentucky every summer and when the July term of court was over, my grandfather joined them. My mother told me that the happiest days of her childhood were spent here, playing in the attic and the hayloft and the water meadows, with a multitude of her Kentucky cousins. But as I looked around I saw nothing that I could accept as a pos-

sible backdrop for all that excitement and mirth and teasing
and tears. There wasn't even a child's swing. The farmer's
wife told us to look around as much as we liked, and went
back to her canning. We paused in the doorway of a long
empty room. I concluded from the parquet floors that it
must have been the drawing room. Since my mother's cousin
had gone to some trouble to bring me here, I felt that I ought
to say something polite, and remarked, "In my great-grandfather's time this must have been a beautiful room," and he
said with a smile, "Grandfather kept his wheat in it." My
uncle may have inherited his *folie des grandeurs* from some
improvident ancestor but it wasn't, in any event, the be-
whiskered old gentleman farmer who built and lived in this
house.

The lessons that hardship had taught my Grandfather
Blinn he was unable to pass on to his son. He must have had
many talks with Ted about his future, and the need to apply
himself, and what would happen to him if he didn't. Hunger
that is only heard about is not very real. My uncle had a
perfect understanding of how one should conduct oneself
after one has arrived; it was the getting there that didn't
much interest him. The most plausible explanation is that
he was a changeling.

From a history of Logan County published in 1911 I learned
that Edward D. Blinn, Jr.—that is, my Uncle Ted—was
the superintendent of the Lincoln Electric Street Railway.
My grandfather must have put him there, since he was a
director and one of the incorporators of this enterprise. One
spur of the streetcar tracks went from the courthouse square
to the Illinois Central Railroad depot, another to a new sub-
division in the northwest part of town, and still another to
the cemeteries. In the summertime the cars were open on

the sides, and in warm weather pleasanter than walking. Except during the Chautauqua season, they were never crowded. The conductor stomped on a bell in the floor beside him to make pedestrians and farm wagons get out of the way, and from time to time showers of sparks would be emitted by the overhead wires. What did the superintendent have to do? Keep records, make bank deposits, be there if something went wrong, and in an emergency run one of the cars himself (with his mind on the things he would do and the way he would live when he had money). The job was only a stopgap, until something more appropriate offered itself. *But what if nothing ever did?*

When my grandfather's back was turned, Ted went to Chicago and made some arrangements that he hoped would change the course of his life; for a thousand dollars (which, of course, he did not have), a firm in Chicago agreed to supply him with an airplane and, in case my uncle didn't choose to fly it, a pilot. It was to be part of the Fourth of July celebration. The town agreed to pay him two thousand dollars if the plane went up.

Several years ago the contract was found tucked between the pages of a book that had been withdrawn from the Lincoln College library—God knows how it got there. It is dated June 27, 1911—to my surprise; for it proves that I was a few weeks less than three years old at the time, and I had assumed that to be able to remember the occasion as vividly as I do I must have been at least a year older than that.

The plane stood in a wheat field out beyond the edge of town. The wheat had been harvested and the stubble pricked my bare legs. My father held me by the hand so I would not get lost in the crowd. Very few people there had ever seen an airplane before, and all they asked was to see this one leave the ground and go up into the air like a bird. Several men in mechanic's coveralls were clustered around the plane. Now and then my uncle climbed into the cockpit and the place grew still with expectation. The afternoon wore on slowly. The sun beat down out of a brassy sky. Word must have passed through the crowd that the plane was not going to go up, for my father said suddenly, "We're going home now." Looking back over my shoulder I saw the men still tinkering with the airplane engine. My father told me a long time later that while all this was going on my grandfather was pacing the floor in his law office, thinking about the thousand dollars he would have to raise somehow if the plane failed to go up, and that if it did go up there was a very good chance his only son might be killed.

Using what arguments I find it hard to imagine (except that a courtroom is one thing and home is another, and drops of water wear away stone), Ted persuaded my grandfather to buy a motorcar. The distance from my grandfather's house to his law office was less than a mile, and the roads around Lincoln were unpaved, with deep ruts. Even four or five years later, when motorcars were beginning to be more common, an automobile could sink and sink into a mudhole until it was resting on its rear axle. But anyway, there it was, a Rambler, with leather straps holding the top down, brass carriage lamps, and the emergency brake, the gearshift, and the horn all on the outside above the right-hand running board. It stood in front of my grandfather's house more like a monument than a means of locomotion. It is unlikely that anyone but Ted ever drove it, and it must have given a certain dash to his courtship of a charming redheaded girl named Alma Haller. I have pursued her and her family through three county histories and come up with nothing of any substance. Her father served several terms as a city alderman, he was a director of the streetcar company, and he owned a farm west of Lincoln, but there is no biography, presumably because he was not cooperative. Anyway, the soft brown eyes, the understanding of what is pleasing to women, assiduousness, persistence, something, did the trick. They were engaged to be married. And if either family was displeased by the engagement I never heard of it.

My uncle had the reputation in Lincoln of being knowledgeable about motors, and a friend who had arranged to buy an automobile in Chicago asked Ted to go with him when he picked it up. On the way down to Lincoln the car skidded and went out of control and turned over. My uncle was in the seat beside the driver. His left arm was crushed and had to be amputated. My grandmother's premonitions were at last accounted for. What I was kept from knowing about and seeing because I was a small child it does not take very much imagination to reconstruct. He is lying in a hospital bed with his upper chest heavily bandaged. There are bruises on his face. He is drowsy from morphine. Sometimes he complains to the nurse or to Annette, sitting in a chair beside his bed, about the pain he feels in the arm that he has lost. Sometimes he lies there rearranging the circumstances that led up to the accident so that he is at the wheel of the car. Or better still, not in the car at all. When the morphine wore off and his mind was clearer, what can he have thought except that it was somebody else's misfortune that came to him by mistake?

When he left the hospital, and forever afterward, he carried himself stiffly, as if he were corseted. He did not let anyone help him if he could forestall it, and was skillful at slipping his overcoat on in such a way that it did not call attention to the fact that his left arm was immovable and ended in a gray suède glove.

A few years ago, one of Alma Haller's contemporaries told me that she had realized she was not in love with Ted and was on the point of breaking off the engagement but after the accident felt she had to go through with it. They went through with it with style. All church weddings that I have attended since have seemed to me a pale imitation of this one. In a white corduroy suit that my mother had made for me, I walked down the aisle of the Episcopal church beside my Cousin Peg, who was a flower girl. I assume that I didn't drop the ring and that the groom put it on the fourth finger of the bride's left hand, but that part I have no memory of; though the movie camera kept on whirring there was no film in it. What was he thinking about as he watched the bridal procession coming toward him? That there would be no more sitting in the moon with girls who had no reason to expect anything more of him than a good time? That there, in satin and lace, was his heart's desire? That people were surreptitiously deciding which was the real arm and which the artificial one? All these things, perhaps, or none of them. The next thing I remember (the camera now having film in it again) is my mother depositing me on a gilt chair, at the wedding reception, and saying that she would be right back. Her idea of time and mine were quite different. The bride's mother, in a flame-colored velvet dress, interested me briefly; my grandmother always wore black. I had never before seen footmen in knee breeches and powdered wigs passing trays of champagne glasses. Or so many people in one house. And I was afraid I would never see my mother again. Just when I had given up all hope, my Aunt Edith appeared with a plate of ice cream for me.

In the next reel, it is broad daylight and I am standing—again with my father holding my hand—on a curb on College Avenue. But this time it is so I will not step into the street and be run over by the fire engines. As before, there is a crowd. It is several months after the wedding. There is a crackling sound and yellow flames flow out of the upstairs windows and lick the air above the burning roof of the house where the wedding reception took place. The gilt furniture is all over the lawn, and there is talk about defective wiring. The big three-story house is as inflammable as a box of kitchen matches.

In the hit-or-miss way of children's memories, I recall being in a horse and buggy with my aunt and uncle, on a snowy night, as they drove around town delivering Christmas presents. And on my sixth birthday our yard is full of children. All the children I know have come bringing presents, and when London Bridge falls I am caught in the arms of my red-haired aunt, and pleased that this has happened. Then suddenly she was not there anymore. She divorced my uncle and I never saw her again. After a couple of years she remarried and moved away, and she didn't return to Lincoln to live until she was an old woman.

As often happened with elderly couples during that period, my grandmother's funeral followed my grandfather's within the year. In his will he named all four of his children as executors, and Ted quit his job with the streetcar company in order to devote himself to settling the estate. My grandfather did not leave anything like as much as people thought he would. He was in the habit of going on notes with young men who needed to borrow money and had no collateral. When the notes came due, more often than not my grandfather had to make good on them, the co-signer being unable to. He also made personal loans, which his family knew about but which he didn't bother to keep any record of since they were to men he considered his friends, and after his death they denied that there was any such debt. Meanwhile, it became clear to anyone with eyes in his head that my uncle was spending a lot of money that could only have come from the estate. My mother and my aunts grew alarmed, and asked my father to step in and represent their interests. He found that Ted had already spent more than half of the money my grandfather left. Probably he didn't mean to take more than his share. It just slipped through his fingers. He would no doubt have run through everything, and with nothing to show for it, if my father hadn't stopped him. My father was capable of the sort of bluntness that makes people see themselves and their conduct in a light unsoftened by excuses of any kind. I would not have wanted to be my uncle when my father was inquiring into the details of my grandfather's estate, or have had to face his contempt. There was nothing more coming to Ted when the estate was finally settled, and, finding himself backed into a corner, he began forging checks. The fact that it didn't lead to his being arrested and sent to prison suggests that the sums involved were not large. I once heard my mother say to my Aunt Edith (who had stopped having anything to do with him) that when she wrote to Ted she was always careful not to sign her full name. The friends whose names he forged were young, in their twenties like my uncle, and poor as Job's turkey. How he justified doing that to them it would be interesting to know. When it comes to self-deception we are all vaudeville magicians. In any case, forging checks for small amounts of money relieved his immediate embarrassment but did not alter his circumstances.

Children as they pass through one stage of growth after another are a kind of anthology of family faces. At the age of four I looked very much like one of my mother's Kentucky cousins. Holding my chin in her hand, she used to call me by his name. Then for a while I looked like her. At the age of eleven or twelve I suddenly began to look like my Uncle Ted. When people remarked on this, I saw that it made my father uneasy. The idea that if I continued to look like him I would end up forging checks amused me, but faulty logic is not necessarily incompatible with the truth, which in this case was that when, because of Christmas or my birthday, I had ten or fifteen dollars, I could always think of something to spend it on. All my life I have tended to feel that money descends from heaven like raindrops. I also understood that it doesn't rain a good deal of the time, and when I couldn't afford to buy something I wanted I have been fairly content to do without it. My uncle was not willing, is what it amounted to.

When my mother died during the influenza epidemic of 1918–19, I turned to the person who was closest to her, for comfort and understanding. I am not sure whether this made things harder for my Aunt Annette or not. Her marriage was rocky, and more than once appeared to be on the point of breaking up but never did. When my Uncle Will came home he would pass through the living room, leaving behind him a sense of strain between my aunt and him, but as far as I could make out it had nothing to do with my being there. Sometimes I found my Uncle Ted there, too. I didn't know, and didn't ask, where he was living and what he was doing to support himself. I think it was probably the low point of his life. There was no color in his face. His eyes never lit up or looked inquiringly or with affection at any of the people seated around the dining-room table. If he spoke, it was to answer yes or no to a question from my aunt. That when he and Annette were alone he opened his heart to her as freely as I did I have no doubt.

Defeat is a good teacher, Hazlitt said. What it teaches some people is to stop trying.

Except for the very old, nothing, good or bad, remains the same very long. My father remarried, and was promoted, and we had to move to Chicago. I went to high school there, and my older brother went off to college, at the University of Illinois, in Champaign-Urbana. On the strength of his experience with the streetcar company, my uncle had managed to get a job in Champaign, working for a trolley line that meandered through various counties in central and southern Illinois. Nobody knew him there, or anything about him. He was simply Ed Blinn, the one-armed man at the ticket counter. He kept this job for many years, from which I think it can be inferred that he didn't help himself to the petty cash or falsify the bookkeeping. During the five years that my brother was in college and law school they would occasionally have dinner together. He tried to borrow money from my brother, whose monthly allowance was adequate but not lavish, and my brother stopped seeing him. Once, when Ted came up to Chicago, he invited me to have dinner with him at the Palmer House. Probably he felt that it was something my mother would have wanted him to do, but this idea didn't occur to me; adolescents seldom have any idea why older people are being nice to them. He was about forty and I was fifteen or sixteen, and priggishly aware that, in taking me to a restaurant that was so expensive, he was again doing things in a way he couldn't afford. He had an easier time chatting with the headwaiter than he did in getting any conversation out of me. After we got up from the table he gave me a conducted tour of a long corridor in the hotel that was known as Peacock Alley. I could see that he was in his natural element. I would have enjoyed it more if there had been peacocks. When I followed my brother down to the university I didn't look my uncle up, and he may not even have known I was there.

Some years later, from a thousand miles away, I learned that he had married again. He married a Lincoln woman, the letter from home said. Edna Skinner. He and his wife were running a rental library in Chicago, and she was expecting a baby. Then I heard that the baby died, and they had moved back to Lincoln, and she was working at the library, and somebody had found him a job running the elevator in the courthouse—where (as people observed with a due sense of the irony of it) his father had practiced law.

By that time my father had retired from business and he and my stepmother were living in Lincoln again. When I went back to Illinois on a visit, I saw my Aunt Annette. She was angry at Ted for marrying. Though she did not say so, what she felt, I am sure, was that there were now two children she couldn't let out of her sight. And she disliked his new wife. She said, "Edna only married him because she was impressed with his family." All this, however, didn't prevent my aunt from doing what she could for them. The grocer was given to understand that they could charge things to her account. She did this knowing that my Uncle Will was bound to notice that the grocery bills were padded, and would be angry with her. As he was. She refused to tell the grocer that her brother and his wife were not to charge things anymore, and my Uncle Will, not being sure what the consequences would be if he put a stop to it, allowed it to continue. Also, living in a small town, there is always the question of what people will think. One would not want to have it said that, with the income off several farms and a substantial balance at the bank, one had let one's brother-in-law and his wife go hungry.

I did not meet Edna until I brought my own wife home to Lincoln for the first time. We had only been married three or four months. When we were making the round of family visits, it struck me as not quite decent not to take her to meet Ted and the aunt I had never seen. My father didn't think that this was necessary. Though they all lived in the same small town, my father never had any reason to be in the courthouse or the library, and he hadn't had anything to do with Ted since the days, thirty years before, when he had to step in and straighten out the handling of my grandfather's estate. But I saw no reason I shouldn't follow my own instincts, which were not to leave anybody out. I was thirty-six and so grateful to have escaped from the bachelor's solitary existence that all my feelings were close to the surface. I couldn't call Ted, because they had no telephone, but somebody told me where they were living and we went there on a Sunday morning and knocked on the screen door. As my uncle let us in, I saw that he was pleased we had come. The house looked out across the college grounds and was very small, hardly big enough for two people. Overhanging trees filtered out the sunlight. I found that I had things I wanted to say to him. It was as if we had been under a spell and now it was broken. There was a kind of easy understanding between us that I was not prepared for. I felt the stirring of affection, and I think he may have as well.

Edna I took to on sight. She had dark eyes and a gentle voice. She was simple and open with my wife, and acted as if meeting me was something she had been hoping would happen. Looking around, I could see that they didn't have much money, but neither did we.

I wrote to them when we got home, and heard from her. After my uncle died, she continued to write, and she sent us a small painting that she had done.

Not long ago, by some slippage of the mind, I was presented with a few moments out of my early childhood. My grandfather's house, so long lived in by strangers, is ours again. The dining-room table must have several leaves in it, for there are six or eight people sitting around it. My mother is not in the cemetery but right beside me. She is talking to Granny Blinn about . . . about . . . I don't know what about. If I turn my head I will see my grandfather at the head of the table. The windows are there, and look out on the side yard. The goldfish are swimming through their castle at the bottom of the fishbowl. The door to the back parlor is there. Over the sideboard there is a painting of a watermelon and grapes. No one stops me when I get down from my chair and go out to the kitchen and ask the hired girl for a slice of raw potato. I like the greenish taste. When I come back into the dining room I go and stand beside my uncle. He finishes what he is saying and then notices that I am looking with curiosity at his glass of beer. He holds it out to me, and I take a sip and when I make a face he laughs. His left hand is resting on the white damask tablecloth. He can move his fingers. The catastrophe hasn't happened. I would have liked to linger there with them, but it was like trying to breathe underwater. I came up for air, and lost them.

The view after seventy is breathtaking. What is lacking is someone, *anyone*, of the older generation to whom you can turn when you want to satisfy your curiosity about some detail of the landscape of the past. There is no longer any older generation. You have become it, while your mind was mostly on other matters.

I wouldn't know anything more about my uncle's life except for a fluke. A boy I used to hang around with when I was a freshman in Lincoln High School—John Deal—had a slightly older sister named Margaret. Many years later I caught up with her again. My wife and I were on Nantucket, and wandered into a shop full of very plain old furniture and beautiful china, and there she was. She was married to a Russian émigré, a bearlike man with a cast in one eye and huge hands. He was given to patting her affectionately on the behind, and perfectly ready to be fond of anyone who turned up from her past. I learned afterward that he had been wounded in the First World War and had twice been decorated for bravery. Big though his hands were, he made ship's models—the finest I have ever seen. That afternoon, as we were leaving, she invited us to their house for supper. The Russian had made a huge crock of vodka punch, which he warned us against, and as we sat around drinking it, what came out, in the course of catching up on the past, was that Margaret and Edna Blinn were friends.

Remembering this recently, I looked up Margaret's telephone number in my address book. The last letter I had had from her was years ago, and I wasn't sure who would answer. When she did, I said, "I want to know about my Uncle Ted Blinn and Edna. How did you happen to know her?"

"We were both teaching in the public schools," the voice at the other end of the line said. "And we used to go painting together."

"Who was she? I mean, where was she from?"

"I don't know."

"Was she born in Lincoln?"

"I kind of think not," the voice said. "I do know where they met. At your grandfather's farm, Grassmere."

"My grandfather didn't have a farm."

"Well, that's where they met."

"My grandfather had a client, one of the Gilletts, who owned a farm near Elkhart—I think it was near Elkhart. Anyway, she moved East and he managed the farm for her. It was called Gracelands. Could it have been there that they met?"

"No. Grassmere."

Oral history is a tangle of the truth and alterations on it.

"They had a love affair," Margaret said. "And Edna got pregnant and lost her job because of it."

"Even though they got married?"

"Yes. It was more than the school board could countenance, and she was fired. He quit his job in Champaign and they went to Chicago and opened a rental library."

"I know. . . . What did the baby die of?"

"It was born dead."

Looking back on my uncle's life, it seems to me to have been a mixture of having to lie in the bed he had made and the most terrible, undeserved, outrageous misfortune. The baby was born dead. He lost his arm in that automobile accident and no one else was even hurt. They put whatever money they had into that little rental library in Chicago just in time to have it go under in the Depression.

The oldest county history mentions an early pioneer, Thomas R. Skinner, who came to that part of Illinois in 1827, cleared some land near the town of Mt. Pulaski, and was the first county surveyor and the first county judge. Edna was probably a direct or a collateral descendant. She may also have been the daughter of W. T. Skinner, who was superintendent and principal of the Mt. Pulaski High School. Whatever her background may have been, she was better educated and more cultivated than any of the women in my family, and if she had had money would, I think, have been treated quite differently.

From that telephone call and the letter that followed I learned a good deal that I hadn't known before. Edna worshipped my uncle, Margaret said. She couldn't get over how wonderful, how distinguished, he was. He was under no illusions whatever about himself but loved her. He called her "Baby."

She never spoke about things they lacked, and never seemed to realize how poor they were. She lived in a world of art and music and great literature. He had a drinking problem.

They lived in many different houses—in whatever was vacant at the moment, and cheap. For a while they lived in what had been a one-room Lutheran schoolhouse. They even lived in the country, and Ted drove them into town to work in a beat-up Ford roadster. Whatever house they were living in was always clean and neat. Annette gave them some of my Grandmother Blinn's English bone china, and Edna had some good furniture that had come down in her family —two Victorian chairs and a walnut sofa upholstered in mustard-colored velvet.

Annette and my Uncle Will Bates went to Florida for several months every winter, and while they were away Ted and Edna lived in their house. She loved my Aunt Annette, and was grateful to her for all she had done for them, and didn't know that the affection was not returned.

Margaret found Ted interesting to talk to and kind, but aloof. She had no idea what he was paid for running the elevator in the courthouse. Edna's salary at the library was seventy-five dollars a month. He made a little extra money by selling cigarettes out of the elevator cage, until some town official put a stop to it because he didn't have a license.

My uncle always dressed well. (Clothes of the kind he would have thought fit to put on his back do not wear out, if treated carefully.) Edna had one decent dress, which she washed when she got home from the library, and ironed, and wore the next day. She loved clothes. When she wanted to give herself a treat she would buy a copy of *Harper's Bazaar* and thumb through the pages with intense interest, as if she were dealing with the problem of her spring wardrobe.

She was a Christian Scientist and tended to look on the bright side even of things that didn't have any bright side. She would be taken with sudden enthusiasms for people. When she started in on the remarkable qualities of someone who wasn't in any way remarkable, Ted would poke fun at her. The grade-school and high-school students who came to the library looking for facts for their essays on compulsory arbitration or whales or whatever found her helpful. She encouraged them to develop the habit of reading, and to make something of their lives. Some of them came to think of her as a friend, and remained in touch with her after they left school. At the end of the day, Ted came to the library to pick her up and walk home with her. Margaret didn't think that he had any men friends.

They had a dog, a mutt that had attached himself to them. Whatever Ted asked the dog to do he would try to do, even if it was, for a dog, impossible. Or when he had, in fact, no clear idea of what was wanted of him. He made my uncle laugh. Not much else did.

He must have been in his early sixties when he got pneumonia. He didn't put up much of a fight against it. Edna believed that he willed himself to die.

"Sometimes she would invite me for lunch on Sunday," Margaret said. "Your uncle ate by himself in the other room —probably because there weren't enough knives and forks for three. Having fed him, Edna would get out the card table and spread a clean piece of canvas on it or an old painting, and set two places with the Blinn china. The forks were salad forks, so small that they tended to get lost on the plates. And odd knives and spoons, jelly glasses, and coffee cups from the ten-cent store. Then she would bring on, in an oval silver serving dish, an eggplant casserole, or something she had invented. She was a superb cook, and she did it all on a two-burner electric plate. After the lunch dishes were washed and put away we would go off painting together. There was nothing unusual about her watercolors but her oils were odd in an interesting way. She couldn't afford proper canvas and used unsized canvas or cardboard, and instead of a tube of white lead she had a small can of house paint. She had studied at the Art Institute when they lived in Chicago. I think now that she saw her life as being like that of Modigliani or some other bohemian starving in a garret on the Left Bank. Ted was ashamed of the way they lived. . . . Only once did she ask me for help. She had seen a coat that she longed for, and it was nine dollars. Or it may have been that she needed nine dollars to make up the difference, with what she had. At that time you could buy a Sears, Roebuck coat for that. Anyway, she asked if I would take two paintings in exchange for the money. . . . When I saw her after her heart attack she was lovely and slender— much as she must have looked when she and Ted first knew each other. She spent the last year or so of her life living in what had been a doctor's office. . . . That nine-dollar coat continues to haunt me."

She was buried beside Ted, in the Blinn family plot. My grandfather's headstone is no higher than the sod it is embedded in, and therefore casts no shadow over the grave of his son.

WITH REFERENCE
TO AN INCIDENT
AT A BRIDGE

(FOR EUDORA WELTY)

When I see ten-year-old boys, walking along the street in
New York City or on the crosstown bus, I am struck by how
tiny they are. But at the time I am speaking of, I wasn't very
big myself. So far as I was concerned, the town of Lincoln
was the Earthly Paradise, the apple that Eve prevailed upon
Adam to eat being as yet an abstraction, and therefore to
all intents and purposes still on the tree. I had an aunt and
uncle living in Bloomington, thirty miles away, and for a
time I went to Peoria with my mother to have my teeth
straightened. Those two towns, and Springfield, the state
capital, constituted the outer limits of the known world.
The unknown world, the infinitude of unconscious emotions
and impulses, didn't come up in ordinary conversation,
though I daresay there were some people who were aware
of it.

At twelve I was considered old enough to join the Presbyterian church, and did. In Sunday school and church I
recited, along with the rest of the congregation, "I believe in
the Holy Ghost, the holy catholic church, the communion
of saints, the forgiveness of sins, the resurrection of the
body, and the life everlasting." That any part of this formal

confession was not self-evident did not cross my mind, nor, I think, anyone else's. We said it because it was true, and vice versa.

Twelve was also the age at which I could join the Boy Scouts and I did that, too. There was only one Scout troop in town, and the scoutmaster, Professor C. S. Oglevee, was a man in his early fifties, who taught biology in Lincoln College, and was the official weather observer. He was, as well, an unordained minister and an Elder in the Presbyterian church. The Scouts were all drawn from the Presbyterian Sunday school.

At Scout meeting I said, "A Scout is trustworthy, loyal, helpful, courteous, kind," and so on, with the same fervor that I recited the Apostles' Creed, and downtown I went out of my way to help elderly people across the street who could have managed perfectly well on their own, for the traffic was negligible. A Model A or a Model T Ford proceeding at the speed of fifteen miles an hour or a farm wagon was what it generally amounted to.

In a short while I passed from second-class to first-class Scout, and kept the silver fleur-de-lys on my hat polished, and looked forward to becoming an Eagle Scout, beyond which there were no further pinnacles to climb. In my imagination the right sleeve of my uniform was covered with merit badges from the cuff to the shoulder, and I did accumulate quite a few.

One day, in quest of specialized information of some sort, I went to see Professor Oglevee at home. He lived in a beautiful old mansion out at the edge of town. It had been built by a pillar of the church, whose widow Professor Oglevee was in the position of a son to. The house was set well back from the street, and painted white, and had a porte cochère, and was shaded by full-grown elm trees. The architect who designed it must have had the antebellum mansions of

Georgia and Mississippi in mind. There was no other house in town like it. The white columns along the front had formerly graced the façade of the Lincoln National Bank. In that house I heard the word "whom" for the first time. A woman answering the telephone while a church social was going on outside in the garden said, "To whom do you wish to speak? . . . To *whom?*"—stopping me in my tracks.

On one side of the lawn there was an apple orchard and on the other a pasture with a little stream running through it: Brainerd's Branch. It says something about old Mrs. Brainerd that children could go there without a sense that they were trespassing. In the early spring I used to walk along the stream listening to the musical sound it made, and sometimes stopping to build a dam. Tucked away in a remote corner of the pasture was a one-room clubhouse with a fireplace, which my brother's generation of Boy Scouts had built under Professor Oglevee's direction. Scout meetings were held there, and after the formal business was out of the way we sat around on the floor roasting wienies over the coals and studying the *Scout Manual*.

Professor Oglevee's room was on the ground level of the house, where the floor was paved with uncemented tiles that clanked as you walked over them. To get to his desk by the window we had to thread our way between piles of scientific and nature publications. Afterward he took me outside and explained the mysteries of his rain gauges. He was a walking encyclopedia. With a dozen boys at his heels, all clamoring for his undivided attention, he moved through the woods identifying trees and plants and mosses. He was immensely patient, good-natured, and kind. So clearly so that I felt there was not room in his nature for the unpredictable crankiness and unreasonable severity other grownups exhibited from time to time. If anybody said one word against him, even today, I would get excited. Which means, of course, that I didn't allow for the fact that he was a fallible human being. The flaws that as a fallible human being he must have had nobody ever knew about, in any case. But on one occasion he shocked me. Somebody said "Professor? . . . Professor? . . . Professor, what kind of a tree is this the leaf of?" and he glanced at it and said, "A piss-elm." Though he then apologized for his language, the fact remained that he had said it.

Whose idea it was to organize the Cub Scouts I don't remember, if I ever knew. A great many things seemingly happened in the air over my head. Cub Scouts had to be between ten and twelve years old, and they did not all go to the Presbyterian Sunday school. It was left to the Boy Scouts to lead them. Among the six or eight little boys who turned up for the first meeting was Max Rabinowitz, whose father had a clothing store on a rather dingy side street facing the interurban tracks and the Chicago & Alton depot, and was a Russian Jew. This distinction would not have meant anything to me if it also had not represented a prejudice of some kind on the part of my elders. I suppose it is why I remember Maxie and not any of the others.

There were a dozen or more old families in town who were German Jewish. The most conspicuous were the Landauers and the Jacobses. Nate Landauer ran a ladies' ready-to-wear shop on the north side of the courthouse square, and his brother-in-law, Julius Jacobs, a men's clothing store on the west side of the square. Once a year my father or my mother took my brother and me downtown and we were fitted out by Mr. Jacobs with a new dark-blue suit to wear to church on Easter Sunday.

The school yard had various forms of unpleasantness, but

anti-Semitism was not one of them. In the Presbyterian church, the doctrine of Original Sin was held over our heads, with no easy or certain way to get off the hook. It was hardly to be expected that the Crucifixion was something the Jews could live down. But on the other hand, it was a very long time ago, and the Landauers and the Jacobses were not present. Mrs. Landauer and Mrs. Jacobs both belonged to my mother's bridge club.

At that age, if I thought about social acceptance at all it was as one of the facts of nature. Looking back, I can see that manners entered into it, but so did money. The people my parents considered to be of good families all had, or had had, land, income from property, something beside wages from a job.

The Russian-Jewish family was quite different. They were immigrants, spoke imperfect English, and had only recently passed through Ellis Island. So far as the Lincoln *Evening Courier* was concerned, news that was not local tended to be about a threatened coal strike or calling out the National Guard to quell some disturbance. Very seldom was there any mention of what went on in Europe. I was a grown man before I learned about the pogroms that drove the Rabinowitzes from their homeland. When I try to recall what the inside of Mr. Rabinowitz's store was like, what emerges through the mists of time is an impression of thick-soled shoes, heavy denim, corduroy, and flannel—work clothes of the cheapest kind. The bank held a mortgage on the stock or I don't know Arkansas. The chances are that he held out until the Depression and then went under, along with a great many other people whose financial underpinnings were more substantial.

What made Maxie want to be a Cub Scout? Had he been reading Ernest Thompson Seton and contracted a longing for the wilderness? Or did he, a newcomer, in his loneliness just want to belong to a group, any group, of boys his own age? We taught the Cub Scouts how to tie a clove hitch and a running bowline and how (if you were lucky) to build a fire without any matches and other skills appropriate to the outdoor life. Somebody, after a few weeks, decided that there ought to be an initiation. Into what I don't think we bothered to figure out.

On a Monday night we walked the little boys clear out of town in the moonlight and halted when we came to a bridge. Somebody suggested a footrace with blindfolds on. A handkerchief was included in the official Cub Scout uniform and they all had one. If they had been sent running up the road until we called to them to stop, they might have tripped or bumped into each other and fallen down, but probably nothing worse. I noticed that the bridge we were standing on had low sides that came up about to the little boys' belly buttons. I cannot pretend that I didn't know what was going to happen, but a part of me that I was not sufficiently well enough acquainted with had taken over suddenly, and he/I lined the blindfolded boys up with their backs to one side of the bridge, facing the other, and said, "On your marks, get set, *go!* . . ." and they charged bravely across the bridge and into the opposite railing and knocked the wind out of themselves.

I believe in the forgiveness of sins. Some sins. I also believe that what is done is done and cannot be undone. The reason I didn't throw myself on my knees in the dust and beg them (and God) to forgive me is that I knew He wouldn't, and that even if He did, I wouldn't forgive myself. Sick with shame at the pain I had inflicted, I tore Max Rabinowitz's blindfold off and held him by the shoulders until his gasping subsided.

Considering the multitude of things that happen in any one person's life, it seems fairly unlikely that those little boys remembered the incident for very long. It was an introduction to what was to come. And cruelty could never again take them totally by surprise. But I have remembered it. I have remembered it because it was the moment I learned that I was not to be trusted.

MY FATHER'S FRIENDS

My father died in 1958, a few months after his eightieth—
and my fiftieth—birthday. The day after he was buried, my
stepmother brought out two heavy winter overcoats for me
to try on, and then she and my older brother and I went to
the storeroom above the garage, and she showed me a brown
leather suitcase of my father's, a much more expensive piece
of luggage than I had ever owned. None of this was my idea,
but I nevertheless could feel on my face an expression of
embarrassment, as if I had been caught out in something.
My stepmother was not given to thinking ill of people but
when my brother and I were children he had assumed the
role of the prosecuting attorney. I glanced at his face now;
nothing unkind there. The coats wouldn't have fitted him,
or my younger brother, and since I was named after my
father, the initials on the suitcase were mine, and who would
want a suitcase with somebody else's initials on it? So why
did I feel that I had appeared to be showing a too avid
interest in the spoils?

Later on that afternoon I started out on foot to call on two
of my father's friends who were not well enough to come to
the funeral. The first, Dean Hill, was a man my father went

fishing with. He was also a cousin of my stepmother. He had inherited a great many acres of Illinois farmland, and he had a beautiful wife. Apart from a trip to Biloxi in the dead of winter, they lived very much as other Lincoln people of moderate means did. I had known him since I was a young boy, and never had a conversation with him. When I go home to Lincoln I tend to put aside whatever in my life I suspect would be of no interest to people there, and sometimes this results in my feeling that I am going around with my head in a brown paper bag. But on this occasion I felt I could be my true self. To my surprise I found that he read books. In Lincoln the women put their names down for best-sellers at the desk of the public library, and the men read the evening newspaper. "What the book is about is a matter of indifference to me," Dean Hill said. "I am interested in the writer—in what he is carefully not saying, or saying and doesn't know that he is. What his real position is, as distinct from the stated one. It keeps me amused. All forms of deception are entertaining to contemplate, don't you find? Particularly self-deception, which is what life is largely made up of."

I found myself telling him about my guilty feelings at accepting my father's things, and he nodded and said, "Once when I was sitting in a jury box the judge said, 'Will the defendant rise,' and I caught myself just in time. If one isn't guilty of one thing one is certainly guilty of another is perhaps the only explanation for this kind of irrational behavior. . . . I'm glad you have the coats and the suitcase, and I'm sure your father would be too. Enjoy them." He then went on to speak affectionately of my father. "I have no other friend like him," he said. "I am already beginning to feel the loss. Most people have a hidden side. Your father was exactly what he appeared to be. It is very rare."

I left the house with a feeling of exhilaration. I couldn't

help feeling that my father's part in this old friendship had somehow been handed on to me, like the overcoats and the suitcase. And in fact it had. When Dean Hill and his wife came to New York six months later, he invited me to lunch at the Plaza, and the conversation was easy and intimate. Everything that he had to say interested me because of its originality and wisdom. While living all his life in a very small Middle Western town and keeping his eye on his farms, he had managed to be aware of the world outside in a way that no one else there was. Or at least no one I knew. He was worried about my stepmother. It was a case of the oak and the ivy, he said, and he didn't think she would manage very well without my father. (He was quite right. She was ten years younger than my father, and when he was alive she was perky and energetic and always talking about taking off for somewhere—except that they couldn't, because of his emphysema. After he was gone, the tears she wiped away with her handkerchief were simply followed by more tears. She spent the remaining fifteen years of her life in nursing homes, unable to cope with her sadness.)

I wrote to Dean Hill, and he answered my letters. The last time I saw him, in Lincoln, twenty-eight years ago, I could talk to him but he couldn't talk to me. He had had a stroke. His speech was garbled and unintelligible. He appeared to feel that it was his fault.

My second call, the day after the funeral, was on Aaron McIvor, who for ten years was a golfing companion of my father's. They also occasionally did some business together. Mr. McIvor dabbled in a number of things, including local politics, and he must have made a living out of all this or he would have gone to work for somebody else. Now and then my father would be asked to handle an insurance policy personally, and in doing so he used the name of Maxwell, McIvor & Company as agent.

Though it would be accurate to say that Aaron McIvor was not like anybody else in Lincoln, it would also, in a way, be meaningless, since small-town people of that period were so differentiated that the same thing could have been said of nearly everybody. He had sad eyes and a sallow complexion and two deep furrows running down his cheeks. The tips of his fingers were stained with nicotine and the whites of his eyes were yellowish also, in a way more often found in dogs than in human beings. Nothing that he said was ever calculated to make people feel better about themselves, but he could be very funny.

As I zigzagged the five or six blocks between Dean Hill's house and the McIvors' that afternoon, I was struck by how little the older residential part of Lincoln had changed. A house here or there where no house was before. A huge old mansion gone.

Aaron McIvor's daughter-in-law directed me up the stairs to his bedroom. The ashtray on a chair beside his bed was full of cigarette butts. He looked the same, only old. I didn't stay long and I wished I hadn't gone to see him, because he had things to say against my father that, the day after his funeral, I didn't feel like listening to.

"McIvor is eccentric," my father would say, when his name came up in conversation. It was not something my father would have wanted anybody to say about him. But he did not expect people to be perfect, and Mr. McIvor's eccentricities in no way interfered with the friendship. Because he said so many unflattering things, it was assumed that he was a truthful man. I don't think this necessarily follows. But if you wanted him you had to take him as he was. The caustic remarks were brushed aside or forgiven. And people loved to tell how, when he was courting his wife, he never brought her candy or flowers but simply appeared, in the evening after supper, and stretched out in the porch swing with his head in her lap and went to sleep.

His wife, whom I called "Aunt" Beth, was my mother's closest friend. When I shut my eyes now, I see her affectionate smile, and the way her brown eyes lighted up. People loved her because she was so radiant. It cannot have been true that she was never tired or that there was nothing in her life to make her unhappy or depressed or complaining, but that is how I remember her.

When I was a little boy of six I met her on a cinder path at the Chautauqua grounds one day and she opened her purse and took out a dime and gave it to me. "I don't think my father would want me to take it," I said. My father knew a spendthrift when he saw one, and, hoping to teach me the value of money, he had put me on an allowance of ten cents a week, with the understanding that when the ten cents was gone I was not to ask for more. Also, if possible, I was to save part of the ten cents. "It's perfectly all right," Aunt Beth said. "Don't you worry. I'll explain it to him." I took off for the place where they sold Cracker Jack. And she stands forever, on the cinder path at the Chautauqua grounds, smiling at the happiness she has just set free. I long to compare her with something appropriate, and nothing is, quite, except the goodness of being alive.

The thing about my mother and Aunt Beth was that they were always so lighthearted when they were together. Sometimes I understood what they were laughing about, sometimes it would be over my head. My father and mother were both mad about golf. I used to caddie for my father, and if he made a bad approach shot he was inconsolable. He would pick his ball out of the cup and walk toward the next tee still analyzing what he had done that made the ball end up in a bunker instead of on the green near the flag. You felt he felt that if he could only have lived that moment over again and kept his shoulder down and followed through properly, the whole rest of his life might have been different. And that Aaron McIvor mournfully agreed with him. The two women were unfazed by such disasters. My mother would send a fountain of sand into the air and go right on describing a dress pattern or some china she had seen in a house in Kentucky. When she and Aunt Beth had talked their way around nine holes—usually my father and Mr. McIvor played in a foursome of men—they would add up their scores and sit down on the balcony of the clubhouse until their husbands joined them. Then, more often than not, they would come back to our house for Sunday-night supper. When my mother went out to the kitchen, Mr. McIvor would get up from his chair and follow her with the intent to ruffle her feathers. My mother had no use for the family her younger sister had married into. Perched on the kitchen stool, Mr. McIvor said admiring things about them. How well educated they were. How good they were at hanging on to their money. How one of them found a mistake of twenty-seven cents in his monthly bank statement and raised such Cain about it that the president of the bank came to him finally in tears. How no tenant farmer of theirs ever drew a simple breath that they didn't know about. And so on. My mother would emerge from the pantry with a plate of hot baking-powder biscuits in her hand and her face flushed with outrage, and we would sit down to scrambled eggs and bacon.

In my Aunt Annette's sun parlor there was a wicker porch swing that hung on chains from the ceiling. *Creak . . . creak . . .* Just as if you were outdoors, only you weren't. It was a good place from which to survey what went on in Lincoln

Avenue. Sitting with her arm resting on the back of the swing, my aunt was alternately there and not there, like cloud shadows. Now her attention would be focused on me (for I was twelve years old and I had lost my mother a couple of years before and my father had sold our house and was on the point of remarrying and I needed her), now on a past that stretched well beyond the confines of my remembering. I didn't mind when she withdrew into her own thoughts; her physical presence was enough. One day I saw, on the sidewalk in front of the house, a very small woman in a big black hat. Not just the brim, the whole hat was big, an elaborate structure of ribbon and straw and jet hatpins that she moved under without disturbing.

"Who is *that*?" I asked.

Turning her head, my aunt said, "Old Mrs. McIvor. Aaron's mother. She was born in England."

"Some hat," I said.

"She's been going by the house for many years and I have never seen her without it."

The things I am curious about now I was not curious about then. Where, in that small town of twelve thousand people, did Aaron McIvor's mother live? Did she live by herself? And if so, on what? And what brought her all the way across the Atlantic? And what happened to his father? And how on earth did she come by that hat? None of these questions will I ever know the answer to.

Pre-adolescent boys, at a certain point, become limp, pale, undemanding, unable to think of anything to do, so saturated with protective coloration that they are hardly distinguishable from the furniture, and not much more aware of what is going on around them. I'm not quite sure when Aunt Beth and Mr. McIvor adopted a baby, but it didn't occur to me that any disappointment or heartache had preceded this decision. If I ever saw the baby, lack of interest prevented me from remembering it.

I must have been thirteen or fourteen when I heard that Aunt Beth had cancer and was in the hospital. I felt I ought to go see her. I thought my mother would want me to. My Aunt Annette was in Florida and there was no one to enlighten me about what to expect. I went from room to room of the hospital, reading the cards on the doors and peering past the white cloth screens, and on the second floor, in the corridor, I ran into her. She was wearing a hospital gown and her hair was in two braids down her back. Her color was ashen. She saw me, but it was as if she were looking at somebody she had never seen before. Since then, I have watched beloved animals dying. The withdrawal, into some part of themselves that only they know about. It is, I think, not unknown to any kind of living creature. A doctor passed, in a white coat, and she turned and called after him urgently. I skittered down the stairs and got on my bicycle and rode away from the hospital feeling I had made a mistake. I had and I hadn't. She was in no condition to receive visitors, but I had acquired an important item of knowledge—dying is something people have to live through, and while they are doing it, unless you are much closer to them than I was to her, you have little or no claim on them.

After she was gone, when I rode past her house, I always thought of her. The house had a flat roof and the living-room windows came almost to the floor of the front porch. The fact that there were so few lights burning on winter evenings may have accounted for the look of sadness. Or it could have been my imagination.

For years after we moved to Chicago my stepmother was homesick and we always went down to Lincoln for the holidays so that she could be with her family. One evening, a couple of days after Christmas, I happened to be walking down Keokuk Street, and when I came to the McIvors' house I turned in at the front walk. I don't know what made me do it. Recollection of those Sunday-night suppers when my mother was alive, perhaps, or of my father and Mr. McIvor retiring to my father's den, where he kept the whiskey bottle, for a nightcap. The housekeeper let me in. The little boy—I had almost forgotten about him—who peered at me from behind her skirt must have been six or seven. Mr. McIvor hadn't come home from his office yet, she said, and retired to the kitchen.

I couldn't remember ever having been inside the house before, and I looked around the living room: dark varnished woodwork, Mission furniture, brown wallpaper, brown lampshades. It didn't seem at all likely that after Aunt Beth died Mr. McIvor destroyed all traces of her, but neither did it seem possible that she would have chosen to live with this disheartening furniture. There were brass andirons in the fireplace but no logs on them and no indication that the fireplace was ever used. No books or magazines lying around, not even the *Saturday Evening Post*. The little boy wanted to show me the Christmas tree, in the front window. The tree lights were not on, and he explained that they were broken. The opened presents under the tree—a cowboy suit, a puzzle, a Parcheesi board, and so on—were still in the boxes they had come in. With a screwdriver that the housekeeper produced for me I located the defective bulb, and the colored lights shone on the child's pleased face. The stillness I heard as I stood looking at the lighted tree was beyond my power to do anything about. I said goodbye to the little boy and picked up my hat and coat and left, without waiting for Mr. McIvor to come home.

When I married I took my wife to Lincoln. She was introduced to all the friends of the family, including Aaron Mc-

Ivor, whom she was charmed by. She told me afterward that at one point in their conversation he turned and looked at me and then said, "He's a nice boy but queer—very queer."

When I went to see Mr. McIvor on the day after my father's funeral, his criticism boiled down to the fact that my father liked women too much, and let them twist him around their little finger.

My father was an indulgent husband, but he hated change and was devoted to his habits, and it took a prolonged campaign and all sorts of stratagems on my stepmother's part to get him to agree to enclose the screened porch or buy a new car. In any case, he was not a skirt chaser. So what did all this mean?

I think even more than by what he said I was upset by his matter-of-fact tone of voice—as if my father's death had aroused no feelings in him whatever. There was no question that my father considered Aaron McIvor his friend. Could it be that he disliked my father, and perhaps always had? Or did he dislike everybody, pretty much?

As I listened to him, I wondered if he had been envious of my father—of his success in business, and of the fact that he was, many people would have said, as fortunate in his second marriage as he was in his first. Because Aaron McIvor had made a decision and stuck to it didn't mean that he never considered the alternative. And even a so-so marriage might have been better than the unshared bed and the unending solitude he came home to day after day for something like forty years.

"I don't agree with you," I said, and "I don't think that's right." And he said with a sniff, "I knew him better than you did."

It crossed my mind, after I had left the house, that he

might have been playing with me the game he used to play with my mother. But on those far-off Sunday evenings he had a look of glee in his eyes, where now there was simply animosity. From which it did not appear that I was excluded.

I always assumed he was fond of my mother or he wouldn't have enjoyed teasing her. Was it on her account that he resented the fact that my father had remarried—if he did resent it? If I had had my wits about me, I would have retraced my steps and asked Dean Hill what he thought. He and Aaron McIvor were not, so far as I know, friends, but they had spent a lifetime in the same small town, where everything is known, about everybody. Also, they were direct opposites—the one so even-tempered and observant and responsive to any kind of cordiality, the other so abrasive. And opposites often instinctively understand each other. Whether Dean Hill came up with a believable explanation or not, ambiguity was meat and drink to him, and he would probably have considered the conversation in that bleak upstairs bedroom from angles I hadn't thought of. He might even have suggested, tactfully, that in my being so hot under the collar there just could be something worth looking into. My father and I were of very different temperaments, and he didn't know anything about the kind of life I was blindly feeling my way toward. He had only my best interests at heart, but as an adolescent and in my early twenties I had resented his advice and sometimes taken pleasure in doing the opposite of what he urged me to do.

Instead, I stopped off at my Aunt Annette's. She listened to my account of the visit to Aaron McIvor and did not attempt to explain his behavior, beyond saying he had always been that way. She then told me something I didn't know: "As Beth lay dying, she said to Aaron, 'You are the dearest husband any woman ever had.' "

In the face of that, nothing I had been thinking seemed worth giving serious consideration to. She was his life. There wasn't the faintest chance of his finding another woman like her, and it was not in his nature to make concessions. So he made do with housekeepers, and brought up his son. When he was stumped by something he went to see the old woman with the big black hat, who knew a thing or two about bringing up children (or so I like to think) and who was not put off by anything he said, being of the opinion that his bark was worse than his bite.

THE FRONT
AND THE BACK PARTS
OF THE HOUSE

Though it took me a while to realize it, I had a good father. He left the house early Tuesday morning carrying his leather grip, which was heavy with printed forms, and walked downtown to the railroad station. As the Illinois state agent for a small fire and windstorm insurance company he was expected to make his underwriting experience available to local agents in Freeport, Carbondale, Alton, Carthage, Dixon, Quincy, and so on, and to cultivate their friendship in the hope that they would give more business to his company. I believe he was well liked. Three nights out of every week he slept in godforsaken commercial hotels that overlooked the railroad tracks and when he turned over in the dark he heard the sound of the ceiling fan and railway cars being shunted. He knew the state of Illinois the way I knew our house and yard.

He could have had a much better job in the Chicago office but my mother said Chicago was no place to raise children. When the offer came a second time, ten years later, my father accepted it. He was forty-four and ready to give up the hard life of a traveling man. My stepmother wept at the thought of leaving her family and Lincoln but came to like living in Chicago. They lived there for twenty years. With my future in mind—he wasn't just talking—my father assured me solemnly that you get out of life exactly what you put into it. I took this with a grain of salt; a teacher in my high school in Chicago, a woman given to reading Mencken and *The American Mercury*, had explained to me that there are people who have always drawn the short end of the stick and will continue to. But for my father the maxim was true. He reserved a reasonable part of his life for his responsibilities to his family and his golf game, and everything else he put into the fire-insurance business. He ended up Vice-President in Charge of the Western Department, which satisfied his aspirations. When the presidency was offered to him he turned it down. It would have meant moving East, and he foresaw that in the New York office he would be confronted with problems he might not be able to deal with confidently.

A detached retina brought his career to a premature end. They moved back to Lincoln, to the same street, Park Place, but a different house. I was in my early forties and living in the country, just beyond the northern suburbs of New York City, and trying to make a living by writing fiction, when my father wrote me that it was about time I paid them a visit. He met me at the station, and as we drove into Park Place I saw that time is more than an abstract idea: maple and elm saplings that were staked against the wind when we moved away had become shade trees. I spent the first evening with my father and my stepmother, and next morning after breakfast I walked over to my Aunt Annette's. She was my mother's younger sister, and they were very close. I loved going to her house because nothing ever changed there. When she sold it many years later because the stairs got to be too much for her, I felt the loss, I think, more than she did.

In that house the present had very little resonance. The

things my aunt really cared about had all happened in the early years of her life. My Great-Grandfather Youtsey's farm on the Licking River in Kentucky, where she spent every summer of her childhood, had passed out of the family. The Kentucky aunts and uncles and cousins she was so fond of she was not free to visit anymore. Her father and mother and my mother were all lying side by side in the cemetery.

In the front hall, under the stairs, there was a large framed engraving of the Colosseum, bought in Rome the year I was born. In the living room there were further reminders: Michelangelo's *Holy Family*, the Bridge of Sighs, and a Louis XV glass cabinet full of curios. Lots of Lincoln people had been to Chicago, and some even to New York, but very few had any firsthand knowledge of what Europe was like—except the coal miners, and they didn't count. The sublime souvenirs kept their importance down through time.

Over the high living-room mantelpiece was a portrait-size tinted photograph of my Grandfather Blinn. I could almost but not quite remember him. When I stood and contemplated it I was defeated by the unseeing look that likenesses of dead people always seem to have. My Aunt Annette was his favorite child. To his boyhood on his father's cattle farm near St. Johnsbury, Vermont, and to the obstacles he surmounted in order to become a lawyer, the photograph offered no clue whatever. Nor did it convey what a warmhearted man he was. What it did suggest, if anybody wanted to look at it that way, was that in my uncle's house a dead man was held in greater esteem than he was.

My aunt had made what other members of the family considered a mistaken marriage, which she had long ago stopped discussing with anyone. If she had really wanted to she could have extricated herself from it. It was as if she believed in the irrevocability of choices, and was simply living with the one she had made as a young woman.

My Uncle Will had graduated from Yale with an engineering degree, and held a license to practice surveying, but he also had inherited several farms, and he was gone from six-thirty in the morning until late afternoon, making sure that his tenant farmers didn't do something that might be to their advantage but not his. I guess he was an intelligent man, but if one of the main elements in your character is suspicion, intelligence is more often than not misused. My aunt was a very beautiful woman and he loved her but her beauty was a torment to him. He did not want her to accept invitations of any kind and they never entertained. It upset him if she even went to the Friday-afternoon bridge club, because what if the hostess's husband were to leave his office early and come home?

Annette was alone in the house all day, with no one to talk to but the colored woman in the kitchen. Lula had a great many children and from time to time she quit in order to have another. Sometimes she just quit. Or my aunt fired her because she had failed to show up for too many mornings in a row. She was always eventually asked to come back, because my aunt needed her in the skirmishing that took place with my Uncle Will. The indignant things Annette didn't feel it was safe to say to him Lula, looking him straight in the eye, said. My uncle seldom took offense, perhaps because she was colored and his servant and not to be taken seriously, or perhaps because she was not afraid of him and so had his grudging respect. When my aunt couldn't find her glasses she borrowed Lula's, which, even though there was only one lens and that had a crack in it, worked well enough. And when she felt like crying, Lula let her cry.

Like the house, my aunt changed very little over the years. Her hair turned grey, and she was heavier than she was when I was a child, but her clear blue eyes were still the eyes of a young woman.

I opened the front door and called out and she answered

from the sun porch. My feelings poured out of me, as always when I was with her. Suddenly she interrupted what I was telling her to say, "I have a surprise for you. Hattie Dyer is in the kitchen."

I got up from my chair and for the length of time it took me to go through the house blindly like a sleepwalker I had the beautiful past in my hand. When I walked into the kitchen I saw a grey-haired colored woman standing at the sink and I said "Hattie!" and went and put my arms around her.

I don't know what I expected. I hadn't thought that far. Or imagined what her response might be.

There was no response. Any more than if I had hugged a wooden post. She did not even look at me. As I backed away from her in embarrassment at my mistake, she did not do or say anything that would make it easier for me to get from the kitchen to the front part of the house where I belonged.

If I had acted differently, I asked myself later—if I had been less concerned with my own feelings and allowed room for hers, if I had put out my hand instead of trying to embrace her, would the truce between the front and the back parts of the house have held? Would she have wiped her hand on her apron and taken my hand? And said (whether it was true or not) that she remembered me? And listened politely to my recollections of the time when she worked in our kitchen? And then perhaps I would have perceived that her memories of that time were vague or nonexistent, so that we very soon ran out of things to say?

I didn't tell my aunt what had happened. I was afraid she would say "Why did you put your arms around her?" and I didn't know why. Also, I thought she might be provoked at Hattie, and I didn't want to have to consider her feelings as well as my own.

The next time I was in Lincoln, a year or two later, Lula was back and saw me coming up the walk and opened the front door to me.

Twice a day, with dragging footsteps—for he was an old man—Alfred Dyer came up the brick driveway of our house on Ninth Street to clean out the horse's stall and feed and curry him, and shovel coal into the furnace. His daughter Hattie kept house for my Grandmother Blinn at the end of her life when, immobilized by dropsy, she sat beside the cannel-coal fire in the back parlor, unable to arrive at the name of one of her children or grandchildren without running through the entire list of them. I don't remember ever being alone with her, though I expect I was. Or anything she ever said to me. I was five years old when she died. The day after her funeral my mother sat down at the kitchen table with Hattie and when they had finished talking about the situation in that house my mother asked her if she would like to come across the street and work in ours.

Hattie was a good cook when she came to us and she learned effortlessly anything my mother chose to teach her. She was paid five dollars a week—two hundred and sixty dollars a year, the prevailing wage for domestic servants in the second decade of this century. If you take into consideration the fact that it was one-twelfth of my father's annual salary, it doesn't seem so shocking.

The week took its shape from my father's going away and returning, but otherwise every day was a repetition of other days, with, occasionally, an event intruding upon the serenity of the expected. My older brother came down with chicken pox and I caught it from him. Or we had company. Or the sewing woman settled down in an empty bedroom and, with her mouth full of pins, arranged tissue-paper patterns and scraps of dress material on the headless dress form.

Sometimes my mother's friends came of an afternoon and the tea cart was wheeled into the living room and they sat drinking tea and talking as if their lives depended on it, and I would go off upstairs to play and come down an hour later to find them gone and Hattie washing the teacups.

Monday mornings two shy children that I knew were hers came to the back door with an express wagon and Hattie gave them our washing, tied up in a sheet, for her mother to do. I knew that old Mrs. Dyer's house was on Elm Street, near the intersection at the foot of Ninth Street hill, and I assumed that when Hattie finished the supper dishes and closed the outside kitchen door behind her, that was where she went. It may or may not have been true. After three or four days Mrs. Dyer sent the washing back, white as snow and folded in such a way that it gave my mother pleasure as she put it away in the upstairs linen closet.

There were places in that house that I went to habitually, the way animals repeat their rounds: the window seat in the library, the triangular space behind a walnut Victorian sofa in the living room, the unfurnished bedroom over the kitchen. And if I was suddenly at loose ends because the life had gone out of the toys I was playing with, I would find my mother and be gathered onto her lap and consoled. If she was not home I would wander out onto the back porch and listen to the upward-spiraling sound of the locusts.

The dog went to my mother when he wasn't sure we all liked him as much as it is possible for a dog to be liked, and felt better after she had talked to him. My brother, who was four years older than I, had a running argument with her about whether he was eleven or, as he insisted, twelve. If in the dead of winter my father opened his three-tiered metal fishing box and sorted through the flies, he chose the room where she was to do it in. When summer came she packed a picnic hamper, and my father brought the horse and carriage around to the high curbing in front of the house, and against a disapproving background of church bells we drove out into the country to a walnut grove with a stream running through it. My mother sat on a plaid lap rug and pulled in one sunfish after another, while my father tramped upstream casting for bass. We could have been the only people on earth. I think my mother enjoyed those long drowsy fishing expeditions but in any case she did whatever it made him happy to do. How much he loved her I heard in his voice whenever he called to her. And how much she loved him I saw in her face when he arrived on the front porch on Friday afternoon and we all came out of the house to greet him. As my father stood with his arms around us, the dog wormed his way past my legs so that his presence too would be recognized.

The Christmas holly that the first grade had cut out of red and green paper and pasted on the schoolroom windows was replaced by George Washington's hatchet, which turned up again on the scorecard that my mother brought home to me from her bridge club. When we looked at the teacher we also saw the calendar on the wall behind her desk: April 1, 1915: April Fools' Day.

I have learned to read. I can read sentences out of the evening paper. The big black headlines are often about the war between Germany and the Allies. From the window seat in the library I watch as my father stands and holds an opened-out page of the Lincoln *Evening Courier* across the upper part of the fireplace so the chimney won't smoke. (The war between *us* broke out when I was three or four years old. I woke up in the night with a parched throat and called out—it was by no means the first time this had happened—for a drink. And waited for my mother's footsteps and the bathroom glass against my dry lips. Instead, his voice, from across the hall, said, "*Oh*, get it yourself!") The newspaper catches fire and floats up the chimney, and I pull the curtain around me in order to peer out at the darkness and the piles of snow. In May, where the piles of dirty snow were, the flowering almond is in bloom. It has suckered and spread through the wire fence into the Kiests' yard. Do the flowers on that side belong to them or to us?

D. W. Griffith's *Birth of a Nation* is showing at the movie theater downtown and there are scenes in it that have made all the colored people in Lincoln angry. I am told to stay out of the kitchen.

The sentences we are called on to read out loud in class are longer and more complicated. We have to memorize the forty-eight states and their capitals, and the countries of South America. With a pencil behind his ear, my father goes through an accumulation of inspection slips, making a check mark now and then, and hands them to me to alphabetize. (Spreading them around me on the rug, I am proud to be of help to him.)

Slumped down in her chair, my mother feels with the toe of her shoe for the buzzer that is concealed under the dining-room rug. My brother and I find her searching hilarious. My father wonders why she just doesn't buy a little bell she can ring. In the end she has to give up, and calls out to the kitchen. The pantry door swings open and Hattie appears to clear away the plates and bring the dessert. She too thinks it is funny that the buzzer is never where it is supposed to be.

How many years was she with us? Five, by my calculations. One day I went out to the kitchen for a drink of water and saw her daughter Thelma at the kitchen sink with an apron on. She said she had come to work for us. She was twelve years old but tall for her age. I asked my mother where Hattie was and my mother said, "She's been having trouble with her husband and moved to Chicago." My mother didn't say what the trouble was and I assumed it was one of the things that are not explained to children. But I felt the trouble was serious if Hattie had to go away. And her absence made me aware of an unpleasant possibility: things could change.

To everything that my mother said to Thelma she answered "Yes, ma'am" and "No, ma'am," but as though she were hearing it from a great distance, and she moved with the slowness of a person whose heart is somewhere else. My mother detected a film of grease on all the dishes and spoke to her about it. When there was no improvement, she decided that Thelma wasn't ever going to be like Hattie, and let her go.

The good-natured farm girl who was in our kitchen after that was taking classes at night so she could pass an examination and work in the post office. My mother was satisfied with her but spoke regretfully of Hattie, who knew what she wanted done without having to be told.

The school calendar has marched straight on to the fall half of the year 1918. We have learned how to do long division. The women who come to our house in the afternoon put their teacups aside and hem diapers as they sit gossiping. They all know what my mother has told me in confidence, that I am going to have a baby brother or a baby sister. They also know—in a small town there was no way for such a thing not to be known—that my mother had a difficult time when my older brother was born, and again with me. Only my Aunt Annette knew that at this time she had premonitions of dying.

My mother hopes that the baby will be a girl, and I am sure that what my mother wants to have happen will happen. Nothing turned out the way anybody hoped or expected it to. My younger brother was born in a hospital in Bloomington during the height of the epidemic of Spanish influenza. Toward the end of the first week in January, Alfred Dyer, coming up the driveway to tend the furnace, cannot have failed to see the funeral wreath on the door.

There is no cure but time. One of my mother's friends said that, putting her hand on my father's shoulder as he sat, hardly recognizable, in his chair. I thought about my mother in the cemetery and wondered if she would wake up and try to get out of her coffin and not be able to. But children have to go to school no matter what happens at home. I learned that the square root of sixty-four is eight, and that π is 3.14159 approximately, and represents the ratio of the circumference to the diameter of a circle.

Years passed without my thinking about Hattie Dyer at all, and then suddenly there I was backing away from her in confusion. When I told my wife about it she said, "It wasn't Hattie you embraced but the idea of her." Which was clearly true, but didn't explain Hattie's behavior.

Because my mother was fond of her it doesn't necessarily follow that Hattie was fond of my mother. My mother may have been only the white woman she worked for. But if this were true I think I would have sensed it as a child. Perhaps —it was so long ago—she neither remembered nor cared what my mother was like by the time I put my arms around her in my aunt's kitchen.

If I had had the courage to stand my ground and say to her, "Why do you refuse to admit that you knew me when I was a little boy?" I don't think she would have given me any answer. However, people do communicate their feelings helplessly. Jealousy can be felt even in the dark. Lovers charge the surrounding air with their delirium. What I felt as I backed away from that unresponsive figure was anger.

. . .

My Aunt Edith was married to a doctor and lived in Bloomington. They had no children and she wanted to take the baby when my mother died, but my father clung to the belief that my mother would have wanted him to keep the family together and not let my brothers and me grow up in separate households, no matter how loving. We were too young to shift for ourselves while he was away, and what he needed was a woman who knew how to run a house and take care of a baby. Hattie could have managed it with one hand tied behind her. So could Annette's Lula. And they would have brought life into the house with them. I cannot believe that there were no more colored women like them in Lincoln. But he thought (and so did everybody else) that he had to have a white woman. The first housekeeper was hired because she had been a nurse. She had nothing whatever to say, not even about the weather. She had never been around children before, and I felt no inclination to lean against her.

My brother and I struggled against the iron fact that my mother wasn't there anymore. Or ever going to be. Tears did not help. The house was like a person in a state of coma. If Annette had not turned up sometime during every day I think we would all have stopped breathing. Any domestic crisis that arose remained undealt with until my father came home. He never knew when he left the house on Tuesday morning what brand-new trouble he would find when he returned on Friday afternoon. My mother's clothes closet was empty. Her silver-backed comb and brush and hand mirror were still on her dressing table, but without the slight disorder of hairpins, powder, powder puff, cologne, smelling salts, and so on, they were reduced to being merely objects. How endless the nights must have been for him, in the double bed where, when he put out his hand, it encountered only the cold sheets.

The first housekeeper lasted three months. The second took offense no matter which way the wind blew, and it would have been better to have no one. She made mischief between the two sides of the family and was dismissed when she developed erysipelas. The farm girl passed her examination and gave notice. And so it went. Each time my father's arrangements collapsed he turned in desperation to old Mrs. Dyer, and though she was crippled with rheumatism she came and fed us until he found someone to take over from her.

During this period he made an appointment with the local photographer. The result is a very strange picture. My father sits holding the baby on his lap. The baby looks uncomfortable but not about to cry. My father is wearing a starched collar and a dark-blue suit, and looks like what he was, a sad self-made man. My older brother has a fierce expression on his face, as if he means to stare the camera out of countenance. I am standing beside him, a thin little boy of ten, in a Norfolk jacket, knee pants, and long black stockings. The photographer was a man with a good deal of manner, and as he ducked his head under the black cloth and then out again to rearrange the details of our bodies I was threatened with an attack of the giggles, which would not have been appropriate, because my father meant the picture to be a memorial of our bereavement.

Annette and her husband were in the habit of spending the winter in Florida. The first Christmas after my mother's death she sent him and my Cousin Peg down South without her so she could be with us. Shortly after that I became aware of conversations behind closed doors and then somebody forgot to close the door. Out of fury because she had been dismissed, the second housekeeper had written several unsigned poison-pen letters to my Grandmother Maxwell, in which she said that my father was carrying on with my Aunt Annette. My Uncle Will Bates received similar letters. His response was to put a stop to Annette's coming to our house at all.

My brother felt that it would be disloyal to my father if he set foot in my uncle's house. Nothing on earth (and certainly not the awkwardness) could have kept me from being where Annette was. What I didn't tell her about my feelings she seemed to know anyway. She told Lula to put an extra place at the table for me, and made me feel loved. She also got me to accept (as far as I was able at that age to do this) the succession of changes that came about, a year later, when my father's grief wore itself out and he put his life with my mother behind him. Children, with no conception of how life goes on and on, expect a faithfulness that comes at too high a price. Now that I am old enough to be his father I have no trouble saying yes, of course he should have remarried. He had always liked women, and without feminine companionship, without someone sitting at the opposite end of the table whom he could feel tenderly about, he would have turned sour and become a different man. He began to accept invitations, and the matchmakers put their heads together.

There used to be, and probably still is somewhere, a group picture of the guests at my father's wedding, which took place in the house of my stepmother's sister, in 1921. The photographer set up his tripod and camera on the lawn in front of the house, and as the guests assembled in front of him there was a good deal of joking and laughter. I had already passed over the line into puberty but not yet reached the stage of hypercritical judgments when I would find the loud laughter of a room full of grown people enjoying themselves unbearable.

During the years that my father lived in Chicago his heavy leather grip, that my mother had hated the sight of, remained on a closet shelf unless we took the train down to Lincoln. There were several people he felt obliged to call on whenever he went home, and one of them was Mrs. Dyer, who still lived in the little house at the foot of Ninth Street hill. He expected his sons to go with him. The visits went on as long as she lived. Mr. Dyer was never there, and I think must have died. I was not expected to take part in the conversation; only to be there. And so my eyes were free to roam around the front room we sat in. The iron potbellied stove, the threadbare carpet, the darkened wallpaper. The calendar, courtesy of the local lumber company. The hard wooden chairs we sat on. Mrs. Dyer and my father talked about her health, about changes in Lincoln, about how fast time goes. And then he made some excuse that got us on our feet. As we were saying goodbye he took out his billfold and extracted a new ten-dollar bill. But not one word did either of them say about the thing that had brought him there, which was that in the time of his greatest trouble, when there was no one else he could have turned to, she didn't fail him.

In a box of old papers, not long ago, I found an eighty-page history of the town of Lincoln, published by Feldman's Print Shop, in 1953, when Lincoln was celebrating the hundredth anniversary of its founding. Thumbing through it I came upon a picture of Mrs. Dyer, looking just the way I remembered her. She was beautiful as an old woman, and probably always. In the photograph she is wearing a black silk dress with a lace collar. Her mouth is sunken in with age, but her eyes are as bright as a child's, and from her smile you'd think it had been a privilege to stand over a tub of soapy water doing other people's washing year in and year out. Surrounding the picture there is an interview with Hattie, who had been chosen as "a respected citizen of the community" to give "something of the history of one of our distinguished colored families." The interview is only five hundred words long, and I assume that much of what she said never got into print. For example, what about her brother Dr. William Dyer? Was the interviewer unaware that he had succeeded in becoming a doctor when this was exceedingly rare for a Negro and that he was on the surgical staffs of the best hospitals in Kansas City? Or that he was also among those citizens of Lincoln who were especially honored at the centennial celebration? Perhaps the history went to press before this fact was known. In any case, while Dr. Dyer was in town for the honoring he stayed with her. He had managed to put himself in a position where no white man could summon him with the word "Boy!" She must have been immensely proud of him. The interview does quote Hattie as saying that in Alfred Dyer's house "there were no intoxicants allowed, no dancing, no card playing, but how we loved to dance! And we did dance when they were away from home." As long as her father was able to work, Hattie said, he was employed by the B. P. Andrews Lumber Company in town. I suspect he had many jobs, some of them overlapping. It is hard to believe how little people were paid for their labor in those days, but the Dyers managed. They didn't have to walk along the railroad right-of-way picking up pieces of coal. In the interview, Hattie said she was a year old when she was brought to the house on Elm Street.

When her mother first came to Lincoln from Missouri, she worked in a boardinghouse run by a Mrs. Jones, Hattie said. It was on the site of the high school—which, in the twenties, when I went there, was an old building with deep grooves in the stairs worn by generations of adolescent feet. Mrs. Jones's establishment must have ceased to exist a very long time ago. If you have ever eaten in a boardinghouse you know every last one of them. The big oak dining-room table with all the leaves in it, and barely enough room for the thin young colored woman to squeeze between the chair backs and the sideboard. No sooner were the dishes from the midday meal washed and put back on the table and the pots and pans drying upside down in a pyramid on the kitchen range than it was time to start peeling potatoes for supper. Jesus loved her and that got her back on her feet when she was too tired to move. And before long, Alfred Dyer was waiting at the kitchen door to take her to prayer meeting.

"In looking back over the years," Hattie said to the interviewer, "I am proud of my father and mother, who were highly regarded by all who knew them, white as well as black. Their deep religious faith has been my help and strength throughout my life."

During one of those times when my father was searching for a housekeeper and Mrs. Dyer was in our kitchen, she stopped me as we got up from the table at the end of dinner and asked if I'd like to go to church with her to hear a choir from the South. It was a very cold night and there was a white full moon, and walking along beside Mrs. Dyer I saw the shadows of the bare branches laid out on the snow. Our footsteps made a squeaking sound and it hurt to breathe. The church was way downtown on the other side of the courthouse square. As we made our way indoors I saw that it was crammed with people, and overheated, and I was conscious of the fact that I was the only white person there. Nobody made anything of it. The men and women in the choir were of all ages, and dressed in white. For the first time in my life I heard "Swing Low, Sweet Chariot," and "Pharaoh's Army Got Drownded," and "Were You There When They Crucified My Lord?" and "Joshua Fit de Battle of Jericho." Singing "Don't let nobody turn you round," the choir yanked one another around and stamped their feet (in church!). I looked at Mrs. Dyer out of the corner of my eye. She was smiling. "Not my brother, not my sister, but it's me, *O Lord!*" the white-robed singers shouted. The people around me sat listening politely with their hands folded in their laps, and I thought, perhaps mistakenly, that they too were hearing these spirituals for the first time.

I could have asked my aunt about Hattie and she would have told me all that a white person would be likely to know, but I didn't. More years passed. I found that I had a nagging curiosity about Hattie—about what her life had been like. Finally it occurred to me that my Cousin Tom Perry, who lives in Lincoln, might be able to learn about her. He wrote back that I had waited too long. Among white people there was nobody left who knew her, and he couldn't get much information from the black people he talked to. He did find out that when she moved back to Lincoln, she lived in the little house on Elm Street. Tom was in high school with her son, who was an athlete, a track star. He became an undertaker and died in middle age, of cancer of the throat. Hattie spent the last years of her life in Springfield with one of her daughters. Her son was born after Hattie came back to Lincoln to live, and his last name was Brummel, so whatever the trouble with her husband was, they stayed together.

In his letter my cousin said that at the time of his death Alfred Dyer owned his own house and the houses on either side of it. This surprised me. He did not look like a property owner. All three houses were torn down recently, Tom said, and the site had not been built on.

I have not been inside our house on Ninth Street since I was twelve years old. It was built in the eighteen-eighties, possibly even earlier. The last time I drove past it, five years ago, I saw that the present owners had put shutters on the front windows. Nothing looks right to me that is not the way I remember it, but it is the work of a moment, of less time than that, to do away with the shutters and bring back into existence the lavender-blue clematis on the side porch and the trellis that supported it, the big tree in the side yard that was killed by the elm blight, the house next door that burned down one night twenty-five or thirty years ago.

Though I know better, I half believe that if the front door of our house were opened to me I would find the umbrella stand by the window in the front hall and the living-room carpet would be moss green. Sometimes I put myself to sleep by going from room to room of that house, taking note of my father's upright piano with the little hand-wound Victrola on it, Guido Reni's *Aurora* over the living-room mantelpiece, the Victorian sofas and chairs. I make my way up the front stairs by the light of the gas night-light in the upstairs hall, and count the four bedroom doors. Or I go through the dining room into the pantry, where, as the door swings shut behind me and before I can push open the door to the brightly lit kitchen, I experience once more the full terror of the dark. Beyond the kitchen is the laundry, where the big iron cookstove is. Opening off this room are two smaller rooms, hardly bigger than closets. One contains jars of preserved fruit and vegetables and a grocery carton full of letters to my mother from my father. The other room is dark and has a musty odor. The dog sleeps here, on a square of old dirty carpet, and there is a toilet of an antiquated kind. Hattie is expected to use this toilet and not the one in the upstairs bathroom that we use. You could argue, I suppose, that some such arrangement would have been found in other old houses in Lincoln, and because it was usual may not have given offense—a proposition I do not find very convincing.

My mother was thirty-seven when she died. When I try

to recall what she was like, I remember what a child would remember. How she bent over the bed and kissed me good night and drew the covers around my chin. How she made me hold still while she cut my bangs. If I try to see her as one adult looking at another, I realize how much there is that I don't know. One day I heard her exclaim into the telephone "It won't do!" and wondering what wouldn't do I listened. After a minute or two it became clear that a colored family was on the point of buying a house on the other side of the street from ours, and that my mother was talking to somebody at the bank. This in itself was odd. If my father had been home, she would have got him to do it. She must have believed that the matter wouldn't wait until he got home. "It won't do!" she kept repeating into the telephone. "It just won't do." A few weeks later, when a moving van drew up before the house in question, it was to unload the furniture of a white family.

One of the things I didn't understand when I was a child was the fact that grown people—not my father and mother but people who came to our house or that they stopped to talk to on the street—seemed to think they were excused from taking the feelings of colored people into consideration. When they said something derogatory about Negroes, they didn't bother to lower their voices even though fully aware that there was a colored person within hearing distance. Quite apart from what Hattie may have overheard in Lincoln, what she saw and lived through in Chicago, including race riots, might easily have been enough to make her fear and hate all white men without exception. And so in that case it was the color of my skin—the color of my skin and the physical contact—that accounted for what happened in my Aunt Annette's kitchen. Having arrived at this conclusion I found that I didn't entirely believe it, because at the time I had the feeling that Hattie's anger was not a generalized anger; it had something to do with who I was. Did somebody in our family do something unforgivable to her? My Grandmother Blinn? Not likely. My father always leaned over backward to be fair and just toward anybody who worked for him. Though I cannot bring back the words, I can hear, in a kind of replay, the sound of my mother and Hattie talking. We are in the throes of spring housecleaning. Her black hair bound up in a dish towel, my mother stands in the double doorway between the front hall and the living room and directs Hattie's attention to a corner of the ceiling where a spider has taken refuge. With a dust mop on the end of a very long pole, Hattie dislodges it. There is no sullenness in Hattie's voice and no strain in my mother's. They are simply easy with one another.

In the end I decided that I must be barking up the wrong tree, and that what happened in my aunt's kitchen was simply the collision of two experiences. And I stopped thinking about it until I had a second letter from my cousin. "I don't understand it," he wrote. "The colored people in Lincoln have always been very open. If you asked one of them a question you got the answer. This is different. They don't seem to want to talk about Hattie Dyer." In a P.S. he added that the elderly black man who took care of his yard was reading one of my books. Miss Lucy Jane Purrington, whose yard he also looked after, had lent it to him. And in a flash I realized what the unforgivable thing was and who had done it.

From time to time I have published fiction that had as a background a small town very much like Lincoln, or even Lincoln itself. The fact that I had not lived there since I was fourteen years old sealed off my memories of it, and made of it a world I knew no longer existed, that seemed always available for storytelling. Once, I began to write a novel without knowing what was going to happen in it. As the details unfolded before my mind, I went on putting them down, trusting that there was a story and that I would eventually find it. The novel began with an evening party in the year 1912. I didn't bother to make up the house where the party took place because there at hand was our house on Ninth Street and it gave me pleasure to write about it. The two main characters were an overly conscientious young lawyer named Austin King and his wife, Martha, who was pregnant. He had not been able to bring himself to say no to a letter from Mississippi relatives proposing a visit. At the beginning of the novel the relatives have arrived, the party is about to begin, and Martha King is not making things any easier for her husband by lying face down across their bed and refusing to speak to him.

Characters in fiction are seldom made out of whole cloth. A little of this person and something of that one and whatever else the novelist's imagination suggests is how they come into being. The novelist hopes that by avoiding actual appearances and actual names (which are so much more convincing than the names he invents for them), by making tall people short and redheaded people blond, that sort of thing, the sources of the composite character will not be apparent.

We did in fact have a visit of some duration from my Grandmother Maxwell's younger sister, who lived in Greenville, Mississippi, and her husband, their two grown sons, married daughter, son-in-law, and grandchild, a little girl of four. Remembering how their Southern sociability transformed our house, I tried to bring into existence a family with the same ability to charm, but whose ambiguous or destructive natures were partly imagined and partly derived from people not even born at the time of this visit. The little girl crossed over and became the daughter of Austin and

Martha King. The young woman of the invented family was unmarried, and an early feminist, and without meaning to she whittled away at the marriage of her Northern cousin, whom she had fallen in love with. Though I did my best to change my Mississippi relatives beyond recognition, many years later my father told me that in one instance I had managed to pin the donkey's tail on the part of the animal where it belonged. But it was wholly by accident. If you turn the imagination loose like a hunting dog, it will often return with the bird in its mouth.

About fifty pages into the writing of the novel I had a dream that revealed to me the direction the story was trying to take and who the characters were stand-ins for. My father was musical, and could play by ear almost any instrument he picked up, and once had the idea of putting on a musical comedy with local talent. The rehearsals took place in our living room. He sat at the piano and played the vocal score for the singers. My mother sat on the davenport listening and I sat beside her. Things did not go well. The cast was erratic about coming to rehearsals, the tenor flagrantly so. One rainy evening only one member of the cast showed up, the pretty young woman who had the soprano lead. She and my father agreed that there was not much point in going on with it. Two and a half years after my mother's death she became my stepmother. It is not the sort of thing that is subject to proof, but I nevertheless believe, on the strength of the dream and of the novel I had blindly embarked on, that I caught something out of the air—a whiff of physical attraction between the young woman and my father. And since it was more than I could deal with I managed not to think about it for the next twenty-seven years.

Austin King's house was clearly our house, to anyone who had ever been in it. In 1912 Hattie was across the street at my Grandmother Blinn's. But during the visit of my Great-Aunt Ina and her family Hattie was working in our kitchen.

However, I never had it in mind to write about her. Rachel, the colored woman who worked in the Kings' kitchen, was imaginary. Insofar as she was modeled on anyone, it was the West Indian maid of a family in New York I came to know years later. They lived in a big old-fashioned sunless but cheerful apartment off upper Madison Avenue. The front door was never locked, and I used to open it often when I was a solitary young man. I forget whether Renée came from Haiti or Guadeloupe. About her private life I knew nothing whatever and I don't think the family she worked for did either.

In a run-down part of Lincoln I once saw a railroad caboose that had come to rest on concrete blocks, in a yard littered with cast-off objects that were picturesque but of no value: a funeral basket, a slab of marble, a broken-down glider, etc. Rachel had to live somewhere, and so why not here? Her five children were not all by the same father but they were all equally beautiful to her. She was easygoing, and perfectly able to be a member of the family one minute and a servant the next, but nobody owned her or ever would. None of this corresponds in any way with the little I know about Hattie Dyer's life and character, but I am afraid that is beside the point. In an earlier, quasi-autobiographical novel, thinking that my father and stepmother would probably not be comfortable reading about themselves, I made the protagonist's father a racetrack tout living far out on the rim of things, and an elderly friend of the family said disapprovingly, "Why did you make your father like that?" So perhaps there is no way to avoid or forestall identifications by a reader bent on making them.

When I was working on the novel about the Kings, it did not occur to me that Hattie would read it or even know it existed. A few women who had known me as a child would put their names on the waiting list at the Lincoln Public Library, one or two at the most might buy it, is what I thought. Men didn't read books. The *Evening Courier* and the Chicago *Tribune* supplied them with all the reading matter they required.

Early on in the writing of the novel the characters took over, and had so much to say to one another that mostly what I did was record their conversation. The difference between this and hallucination is not all that much. One day a new character appeared, and inserted himself retroactively into the novel. He came on a slow freight train from Indianapolis. "Riding in the same boxcar with him, since noon, were an old man and a fifteen-year-old boy, and neither of them ever wanted to see him again. His eyes were bloodshot, his face and hands were gritty, his hair was matted with cinders. His huge, pink-palmed hands hung down out of the sleeves of a corduroy mackinaw that was too small for him and filthy and torn. He had thrown away his only pair of socks two days before. There was a hole in the sole of his right shoe, his belly was empty, and the police were on the lookout for him in St. Louis and Cincinnati."

On the night of the party, while Rachel was still at the Kings', he appeared at her house and frightened the children, one of whom was his. Rachel was not totally surprised when she walked in on him. She had dreamt about him two nights before. When she realized he was not just after money but meant to settle down with them she took her children and fled. I was frightened of him, too, even as he took life on the page. For a week he stayed blind drunk, and as I described how he lay half undressed on a dirty unmade bed, barely able to lift the bottle to his mouth, I thought *Why not?* and let the fire in the stove go out, and the outside door blew open, and in a little while he died of the cold he had stopped feeling.

I have no reason to think that Hattie's husband, Fred Brummel, was anything but a decent man. My mother's statement that Hattie was having trouble with him possibly amounted to no more than that they were of two minds about moving to Chicago. If Hattie did indeed read my book then what could she think but that I had portrayed her as a loose woman and her husband as a monster of evil? And people in Lincoln, colored people and white, would wonder if I knew things about Fred Brummel that they didn't, and if he was not the person they took him for. I had exposed their married life and blackened his character in order to make a fortune from my writing. I was a thousand miles away, where she couldn't confront me with what I had done. And if she accused me to other people it would only call attention to the book and make more people read it than had already. If all this is true (and my bones tell me that it *is* true) then why, when I walked into my aunt's kitchen, should she be pleased to see me?

I do not feel that it is a light matter.

Any regret for what I may have made Hattie feel is no-where near enough to have appeased her anger. She was perfectly right not to look at me, not to respond at all, when I put my arms around her. I must have seen Fred Brummel at one time or another or else why does his name conjure up a slight, handsome man whose skin was lighter that Hattie's? If, now, I were to go out to the cemetery in Lincoln and find his grave (which would take some doing) and sit beside it patiently for a good long time, would I learn anything more than that dust does not speak, to anyone, let alone to a stranger? He was once alive. He married Hattie and they had several children. That much is a fact. It does not seem too much to assume that he was happy on the day she told him she would marry him. And again when he held his first child in his arms. And that he was proud of Hattie, as proud as my father was of my mother. Who are now dust also.

THE HOLY TERROR

My older brother and I shared a room when we were children, and he was so good at reading my mind that it left me defenseless against his teasing. When I learned something that the family was holding back from him and hadn't considered it safe to tell me, either, my first thought was *He will see it in my face!* But by that time he and I were living in different parts of the country and seldom saw each other, and from necessity I had acquired, like any other adult, an ability to mask my thoughts and feelings. His life was hard enough as it was, and there was no question but that this piece of information would have made it more so. The older generation are all dead now, and what they didn't want my brother to know would still be locked up inside me if my brother's heart hadn't stopped beating, one day in the summer of 1985.

The firm mouth, the clear ringing voice, the direct gaze. In a family of brown-eyed or blue-eyed people, his eyes were hazel.

As a small child—that is to say, when he was five years old—he was strong and healthy and a holy terror. Threats and punishments slid off him like water off a duck's back.

My father, with the ideas of his period, believed that children should learn obedience above everything else, but he was new at being a father, and besides, three days a week he wasn't there. My mother was young and pleasure-loving and couldn't say no to an invitation to a card party, and often left my brother with the hired girl, who was no match for him. He was named Edward, after my Grandfather Blinn. My father's sister christened him "Happy Hooligan," after a character in the funny papers, and part of the name stuck. "Look out, Happy, don't do that!" people shrieked, but he had already done it. One afternoon as my mother emerged from the house dressed fit to kill, he turned the garden hose on her. My Aunt Edith, hearing the commotion, opened the screen door and came out to see what was going on, and she too got a soaking. My brother continued to hold the two women at bay until the stream of water abruptly failed: my father had crept around the side of the house to the outdoor faucet. My brother dropped the hose and ran. At that time, my Aunt Annette lived farther down the street and if he got to her he was safe. She was not afraid of anybody and would simply wrap her skirts around him and there he'd be. She was upstairs dressing and heard him calling her, but by the time she got to the front door my father was holding him by the arm, and possession is nine-tenths of the law.

Down through the years, when family stories were being brought out for company, someone was bound to tell the incident of the garden hose, and about how my father's cigars had to be kept under lock and key.

All such outrageous behavior came to an end before Hap had reached his sixth birthday. The year was 1909. My Aunt Annette, driving a horse and buggy, stopped in front of our house. There was something she wanted to tell my mother. As they were talking my brother said, "Take me with you." Annette explained that she couldn't, but he seldom took no for an answer, and started climbing up the back wheel of the buggy in order to get in beside her. She finished what she had to say and flicked the horse's rump with her whip. I was a baby at the time and there is no way I could remember my mother's screams, but even so I am haunted by them.

My brother's left leg was amputated well above the knee. At some point in my growing up I was told, probably by my father, that if the surgeon had been able to leave three or four more inches of stump it would have made a considerable difference in my brother's walking.

By the time I was old enough to observe what was going on around me, my brother had an artificial leg—of cork, I believe, painted an unconvincing pink. When I opened my eyes in the morning there it was, leaning against a chair. I had no conscious feelings about it. It was just something my brother had to have so he could walk. Over his stump he wore a sort of sock, of wool, and the weight of the leg was carried by a cloth harness that went around his shoulders. In the evening after supper my father would give him lessons in walking properly: "If you will only lead with your wooden leg instead of dragging it behind you as you walk, it won't be noticeable." This was *almost* true. But when Hap was tired he forgot. It has been more than seventy years since we were boys together in that house, but my shoulder remembers the weight of his hand as we walked home through the dusk. If he saw someone coming toward us, the hand was instantly withdrawn.

In the earliest picture of my brother that I have ever seen, taken when he was a year old, he is sitting astride Granny Blinn's shoulders. He was her first grandchild and the apple of everybody's eye. As soon as he was old enough to walk he wanted to be with the men, where the air was blue with cigar or pipe smoke and the talk was about horses and hunting dogs, guns and fishing tackle. Between my Grandfather Blinn and my brother there was a deep natural sympathy— the old bear with the cub he liked the smell of. In my mind I see my brother sitting in the front seat of a carriage, studying now the details of the harness on the horse's back and now my grandfather's face for a response to what he is telling my grandfather. And being allowed to hold the reins when they came to a place where the horse was not likely to be startled by any sudden movement from the side of the road. At a very early age he resolved to follow my Grandfather Blinn into the profession of law, and he never deviated from this.

He was nine years old when my grandfather died. My grandmother died that same year, and the house was sold to a family named Irish, from out in the country. They had three boys and a girl, and Mrs. Irish's mother lived with them. I think it is more than likely that before the moving men had finished carrying the Irishes' furniture up the front walk and into the house Hap and Harold Irish had sized each other up and decided it was safe to make the first move. As it turned out, they were friends for life. Harold was a sleepy-eyed boy who noticed things that other people missed. My brother preferred his company to that of any other boy he knew. Harold understood, without having to be told, that my brother could not bear any expression of pity or any offer of help. With intelligence and skill he circumvented his physical handicap. My father and mother never made anything of this, but they cannot have failed to notice that there was very little other boys could do that Hap couldn't do also.

On October afternoons while the maple leaves came floating down from the trees, the boys of the neighborhood played football in a vacant lot on Eleventh Street. The game broke up when they couldn't see the ball anymore. With a smudged face and pieces of dry grass sticking to his clothes, Hap would place himself on the crossbar of Harold's bicycle, which was always waiting for him. He had a bicycle, and could ride it, but to do this with security and élan you need two good legs. Hashing over plays that had miscarried, they rode home to Ninth Street. If other offers of a ride were made, my brother declined them.

In winter when it was still dark I would be wakened by the sound of gravel striking against the window, and Hap would get up from his warm bed and dress and go off with Harold to see if they had caught anything in the traps they had set at intervals along Brainerd's Branch. They had learned from an ad in a boys' magazine that you could get a quarter for a properly stretched and dried muskrat skin, and they meant to become rich. If they waited till daylight they would find their traps sprung and empty. Other boys—coal miners' sons from the north end of town, they believed— also knew about that ad. More often than not it was bitterly cold, and to reach the pasture where the traps were they had to cope with a number of barbed-wire fences half buried in snowdrifts. I am sure, because I used to see it happen on other occasions, that Harold climbed through the barbed wire and walked on, leaving Hap to bend down and hold the wires apart and pull his artificial leg through after him. My mother was forever mending rips in his trousers.

The summer he was fifteen he and I were sent to a Boy Scout camp in Taylorville, Illinois. With the whole camp watching him he climbed up the ladder to the high-diving platform, his cotton bathing suit imperfectly concealing his stump, and hopped out to the end of the board and took off into a jackknife. His life was one long exercise in gallantry. He wanted to make people forget he was crippled—if possible to keep them from even knowing that he was. He wanted to be treated like anyone else but behaved in such a way as to arouse universal admiration. Not leading with his artificial leg but dragging it after him across the clay court, he won the camp tennis singles. It is no wonder so many people loved him.

Before I was old enough to have any recollection of it, my Aunt Edith worked for a time as a nurse in a state asylum for the feebleminded, out past the edge of town. She met there and eventually married a resident physician named William Young, who soon struck out on his own. As a child I loved to sit on one of his size-12 shoes while he walked back and forth talking to my mother about grownup matters. A deep attachment existed between our whole family and this big, easygoing, humorous man, whose hands smelled of carbolic acid and who never said "Not now" to anything any child wanted him to do.

It was he who told me the truth about Hap's accident. I was in my late twenties when this happened. One day when we were alone together he spoke in passing of my brother's "affliction"—of what a pity it was. Out of a desire to make the unacceptable appear less so, I mentioned something I had been given to understand—that the leg had been broken in so many places they had no choice but to cut it off. My uncle looked at me a moment and then said, "It was a simple fracture, of a kind that not once in a hundred times would have required an amputation." After which, he went on to tell me what Hap didn't, and mustn't ever, know.

In those days, their fees being small, doctors commonly eked out their income by dispensing medicine themselves instead of writing out prescriptions. The family doctor in Lincoln, with easy access to morphine, had become addicted to it and should have been prevented from practicing. Uncle Doc, not liking the sound of what he was told over the telephone day after day about Hap's condition, got on a train and came to Lincoln. He saw immediately that the broken bone was not set. He also saw the unmistakable signs of gangrene. And taking my father aside, he told him that the leg would have to be cut off to save my brother's life.

"Your Grandfather Blinn called that doctor in and cursed him all the way back to the day he was born," Uncle Doc said to me. "In my whole life I have never witnessed anything like it."

This may have a little relieved my grandfather's feelings but it did not undo what had happened. My Aunt Edith, more sensibly, went to Chicago and came home with the finest set of lead soldiers money could buy. Cavalry officers wearing bearskin busbies and scarlet jackets. On black or white horses. For many years my brother played with them with passionate pleasure. Nothing could really make up for the fact that he was doomed to spend the rest of his life putting on and taking off that artificial limb, and could never again run when he felt like it, as fast as his two legs would carry him.

Since I was not a natural athlete like my brother, or an athlete at all, it crossed my mind more than once that having an artificial leg would not have been such a great inconvenience to me, because what I liked to do best was to retire to some out-of-the-way corner of the house and read. I even entertained the fantasy of an exchange with Hap. Along with this idea and rather at odds with it was a superstitious fear that came over me from time to time when I remembered that my mother's only brother lost an arm in an automobile accident when he was in his early twenties. Was there a kind of family destiny that would one day overtake me as well?

There was a period in my life when I lay down on a psychoanalyst's couch four times a week and relived the past. Eventually we arrived at my brother's lead soldiers. I begged to be allowed to play with them and my brother invariably said no. He kept them out of my reach, on top of a high bookcase. One day when Hap was out of the house I put a stool on the seat of a straight chair and climbed up on it. I had just got my hands on the box when I heard the front door burst open and my brother called out, "Anybody home?" In my guilty fright I tried to put the box back, lost my balance, and fell. If my mother had not appeared from the back part of the house at that moment, I don't know what my brother would have done to me. Not one horseman survived intact. I see Hap now, sitting on the floor in the living room, gluing a head back on one of them. The horse already had a matchstick for one of its hind legs, so it would stand up. He never forgave me for what I had done. I didn't expect him to.

The Germanic voice coming from a few feet beyond the crown of my head suggested that my brother's accident had been a great misfortune not only for him but for me also; because I saw what happens to little boys who are incorrigible, I became a more tractable, more even-tempered, milder person than it was my true nature to be. About these thoughts that one is told on good authority one thinks without their ever crossing the threshold of consciousness, what is there to say except "Possibly"? In support of the psychoanalytic conjecture, a submerged memory rose to the surface of my mind. At that Scout camp where Hap won the singles tennis championship I was awarded a baseball glove for Good Conduct.

· · ·

Who has that picture of Hap sitting on Granny Blinn's shoulders, I wonder. Or the one of him driving a pony cart. It was a postcard—which means that it was taken by a professional photographer. On the reverse someone had written "Edward, aged seven, at the Asylum." It was an odd choice. Uncle Doc was practicing in Bloomington by that time. Did the family, even so, regard the asylum grounds as home territory? The road to the Lincoln Chautauqua ran alongside them, and driving by with my father and mother I used to stare at the inmates standing with their hands and faces pressed against the high wire netting, their mouths permanently slack and sometimes drooling. Perhaps the photographer wanted the institutional flower beds as a background. In the photograph my brother is wearing a small round cap. The pony and cart were not borrowed for the occasion but his own. He is holding the reins, and the pony is, of course, standing still. My brother's chin is raised and he is facing the camera, and the expression on his face is of a heartbreaking uncertainty.

Most children appear to be born with a feeling that life is fair, that it must be. And only with difficulty accommodate themselves to the fact that it isn't. That look on my brother's face—was it because of his sense of the disproportion between the offenses he had committed and the terrible punishment for them? Was he perhaps bracing himself for a second blow, worse than the first one? Or was it because of what happened to him when he left our front yard to play with other children? A little boy who couldn't run away from his tormentors or use his fists to defend himself because they were needed for his crutches, and who could easily be tripped and toppled, was irresistible. Since Hap refused, even so, to give up playing with them, my father paid a colored boy named Dewey Cecil to be his bodyguard.

. . .

I assumed, irrationally, that Hap would die before I did; he was older and when we were growing up together he always did everything first, while I came along after him and tried to imitate him when it was at all possible. During the past few years I have often thought, When he is gone there will be no one who remembers the things I remember. Meaning the conversations that took place in the morning when he and I were dressing for school. The time we had chicken pox together. The way the light from the low-hanging red-and-green glass shade fell on all our faces as we sat around the dining-room table. The grape arbor by the kitchen door. The closet under the stairs. The hole in the living-room carpet made by the rifle he said wasn't loaded. The time I tried to murder him with a golf club.

We were waiting for my father to finish his foursome, and for lack of anything better to do Hap threw my cap up in a tree, higher than I could reach. I picked up a midiron and started after him. With a double hop, a quick swing with his bum leg, and another double hop he could cover the ground quite fast, but not as fast as I could. I meant to lay him out flat, as he so richly deserved. Walter Kennett, the golf coach, grabbed me and held me until I cooled down.

My brother didn't mind that I had tried to kill him. He always liked it when I showed signs of life.